A NOTE FROM CADE MERRILL

In 1994 three college students went into the woods near Burkittsville, Maryland, to make a film about the legend of the Blair Witch.

They never came back.

My cousin Heather Donahue was one of those filmmakers. Heather was my favorite cousin—almost like a big sister. When she disappeared, I was only eleven years old. I couldn't accept that she was gone. Was she really dead? Was there actually a Blair Witch? I needed to find answers.

So I read every story about the Blair Witch legend that I could get my hands on. I e-mailed and called everyone who might know something about Elly Kedward, the eighteenth-century outcast some believed to be the Blair Witch, or Rustin Parr, the 1940s serial murderer who claimed that an old woman in the woods had forced him to torture and kill seven children.

It wasn't long before more people heard about my work and started sending their stories to my Web site **theblairwitchfiles.com**. Stories of strange disappearances, of family curses, of ghastly unexplained deaths. The tales are all different, but they always lead back to the Blair Witch. I researched and archived the most intriguing stories in these case files, and sealed them so that no one could exploit them for commercial or sensationalistic purposes.

The discovery of Heather's video footage in 1995 left me with more questions than answers. But it did confirm what I had come to believe—that there is something strange, something incredibly terrifying, in the Blair Woods. And its evil lives on. . . .

I am seventeen now. My case files have grown to thousands of pages. I have decided to open some of them and publish them. Why? Because I know that the answers are out there. My hope is that these books may reach that one person who holds the missing piece—the key that will unlock the mystery of the Blair Witch. If you are that person—or if you have information that may help me find the truth—please get in touch. I can be reached at **theblairwitchfiles.com**. I'm always there.

Cade Merrill

Burkittsville, MD
July 2000

THE BLAIR WITCH FILES #2

THE DARK ROOM

by Cade Merrill

A Parachute Press Book

BANTAM BOOKS
NEW YORK • TORONTO • LONDON • SYDNEY • AUCKLAND

RL: 6.0, AGES 012 AND UP

THE DARK ROOM

A Bantam Book/August 2000

Books created and produced by Parachute Publishing, L.L.C.,
distributed by Random House Children's Books.
© 2000 Artisan Pictures Inc. All Rights Reserved.

The "Stickman" is the registered trademark and service mark of
Artisan Pictures Inc. All Rights Reserved.
Cover art copyright © 2000 by Parachute Publishing, L.L.C.

ISBN: 0-553-49363-9

Visit us on the Web! www.randomhouse.com/teens
Educators and librarians, for a variety of teaching tools, visit us at
www.randomhouse.com/teachers

Published simultaneously in the United States and Canada

Bantam Books is an imprint of Random House Children's Books, a division of
Random House, Inc. BANTAM BOOKS and the rooster colophon are registered
trademarks of Random House, Inc. Bantam Books, 1540 Broadway, New York,
New York 10036.

PRINTED IN THE UNITED STATES OF AMERICA

OPM   10   9   8   7   6   5   4   3   2   1

FOR THE PERSON WITH THE
KEY—WHOEVER YOU ARE

Acknowledgments

I would like to express my heartfelt thanks to Megan Stine for her assistance in the preparation of this manuscript—a major undertaking! I'd also like to thank Ferrell McDonald, Ben Rock, and Amorette Jones. And Ellen Steiber, wherever you are: thanks a million!

THE DARK ROOM

Introduction

One cool thing about having your own Web site is that you never know who's going to fall into your life.

Half the time it's some jerk who wants to waste your time telling you about a weird dream he had—or someone else who makes you chase after some stupid ghost he's hoaxed up.

But every once in a while, you open an e-mail from someone with the power to change your life. Someone you're willing to bend the rules for. Someone who makes you question everything you ever believed to be true.

That's what happened with Laura Morely.

Just typing her name brings back dark images that I would rather forget. But I can still see the look of excitement in her blue eyes and the wide, confident smile she wore the day she arrived in Burkittsville. She was so happy. *Then*.

But this isn't the way a case file is supposed to start. It's getting way too personal.

Let me start over.

Laura Morely fell into my life last summer the way most of my Blair Witch case files do—with an e-mail to my Web site, **www.theblairwitchfiles.com**.

```
TO: Cade@theblairwitchfiles.com
FROM: justin@hotmail.xxxx
RE: Blair Witch

Cade,
    Love your site. Your research is
fantastic. You must be an amazing
person. I totally admire someone
who has a passion for something
and follows it.
    So anyway, I'm a Blair Witch
freak myself. I was born near
Burkittsville (I live in Minnesota
now), and I was interested in the
Blair Witch legend even before
Heather Donahue and the others
disappeared. (Sorry about that. I
know she's your cousin.) Maybe
```

she's still out there somewhere. I mean, is it really possible to get *that* lost in the Black Hills? And where were Heather and Mike at the end of their film footage—does that house really exist? If we looked for it, could we find it? It probably sounds like I'm just another thrill seeker, but it's more than that. I just have to know how it *feels* to be there. I'm not a sick person! I don't know why it's so important to me. It just *is*.

So here's my big question: Could you help me find a place to stay in B-ville this summer? I'm taking the summer off after graduation, and I want to spend some time in the Black Hills area. I've got some serious camera equipment (majoring in photography at college next year—don't tell my parents! They think I'm premed), and I want to take some pictures of the site where Heather disappeared. This may sound crazy, but I feel like I've got some sort of bond with her.

And, to tell you the truth, I'd love to get to know you. You seem like a really cool guy.

Any ideas?

Thanks,
Laura Morely

I almost deleted that e-mail on the spot. I didn't need some girl raving about my fabulous site. It felt like she was kissing up to me. It was obvious that Laura Morely didn't have any new information to offer. Nothing on the Blair Witch or anything connected to the legend.

I figured she was just a girl somewhere in the Midwest who wanted to cruise the area, like everyone else these days. Big deal.

Besides, I couldn't actually think of a decent place for her to stay. But something about her excitement appealed to me. I e-mailed her back and told her there was a motel outside of town, the Wishing Well, but it was a dump. And the rates were outrageous, ever since tourists started streaming into town a few years ago, chasing after the Blair Witch legend. She'd be better off staying home.

A few days later Laura sent me another e-mail, just a quick note. She said the Wishing Well sounded fine to her. She was coming, and could we meet sometime.

Sure, I replied. We can meet if you want. Give me a call. But I didn't give her my phone number. At least, I don't remember giving it to her.

Then the first week of July, the phone rang early on Friday afternoon. I thought it was my parents checking in—they were out of town on a vacation.

But it was Laura.

"Hi," she said. "This is Laura Morely. Remember me?"

To tell you the truth, I didn't. Not at first, anyway. "Uh, remind me," I said.

She sounded surprised. "I e-mailed you a few months ago, about coming to Burkittsville?"

"Oh, yeah," I said. "Sorry, I get tons of e-mail. Hi. So where are you?"

She started talking really fast. "Well, I flew into Baltimore and took a bus to Frederick. Then I took your advice and got a taxi to the Wishing Well. That's where I am now. When I called them last week, they said they had lots of rooms available. But now I find out they haven't got any rooms at all. At least not this week. And God, this place is depressing! I'm here with all this camera equipment, and I'm dead tired—I had to get to the airport at six A.M. to catch my flight!—and I don't know anyone else in this town. And this is so *not* how I wanted my trip to turn out. I don't know what I'm going to do."

I wasn't sure what she should do, either. So I didn't respond right away.

"Listen," she went on, "if there's really no other place to stay around here, I'd probably better get myself back to Minnesota. It's such a bummer. I've been wanting to see Black Hills Forest for years. And now I'm so close, and—"

I was feeling sorry for her, I guess. Because without really meaning to, I said, "I can give you a ride back to Frederick if you want."

"Really?"

"No problem," I told her. "I'll be at the Wishing Well in twenty minutes."

"Fabulous." Her voice was suddenly bouncy, happy, can't wait.

I shook my head and grabbed the keys to my car. Providing cab service is not my usual line. What am I getting myself into? I wondered. This girl was a total stranger. And she had absolutely nothing to add to my Blair Witch investigation.

Or so I thought.

The rest of this book is the case file on Laura Morely. Some of the events I witnessed firsthand, some of them I heard about from Laura herself and from a journal she kept, and others I discovered from independent sources. This is the case that pulled me in so deep, I almost never made it out again. Although I've tried to maintain my objectiv-

6

ity, I don't know if I succeeded. But I saw enough to piece together some facts. As to the truth—you decide.

How much of what happened in those weeks was the work of supernatural forces? How much was even real? I have my own opinions . . . but for now, I'll let the file speak for itself in *The Dark Room*.

PART I:

Laura's Photographs

*Based on historical research and notes
by Cade Merrill*

1

Twenty minutes after getting Laura's call, I pulled up in front of the Wishing Well. The first *W* on the neon sign was broken, so it read *ishing Well Motel*. The place was such a dive. No wonder it depressed her.

Laura wasn't hard to spot. A teenage girl was standing in front of the motel with a big backpack and about four camera bags.

"Hi," I said. I opened the front door of my car, leaned across the seat, and held out my hand. "I'm Cade Merrill."

"Laura Morely," she said, shaking my hand and giving me a megawatt smile. She had stiff blond hair that was chopped off at different lengths, sort of hacked-looking but cool. Her eyes were an amazing robin's-egg blue. And she had a nice mouth. The kind that could look really serious most of the time—but then every once in a while would break into a smile that said "Isn't life wonderful?" She was wearing jeans and some kind of black and red print top. She had a Nikon 35mm slung over her shoulder.

She immediately grabbed it, put it to her eye, and took my picture.

I laughed and pretended to shield my face.

She glanced doubtfully from her pile of bags to my car. I drive a 1968 Morris Minor. It's a tiny little European car, smaller than a Volkswagen. Two seats in front, none in back, held together by rusted, dark green sheet metal. But it's mine. And it gets me around. Laura didn't get sarcastic about it like the kids in my school. ("Whoa, is that actually a car you're driving—or a roller skate?") But she did say, "Is there going to be room for all my junk in there?"

"Hope so." It took a lot of pushing and shoving, but we finally got all her bags into the Morris Minor.

"It's really nice of you to give me a ride back to the bus station," she said.

"I'm sorry your trip didn't work out," I told her.

She gave me a rueful grin. "It's probably the Blair Witch doing her thing. Making sure no one ever documents whether or not she really exists."

That caught my interest. Mostly because I'm sort

of a fanatic about wanting things documented. There's been so much written about the Blair Witch that doesn't even approach real.

Speculation and theories are interesting, but personally, I'm not willing to believe anything until I have documented proof.

"So you wanted to document—?"

"I don't know what exactly," she admitted. "But I figured if I went into Black Hills Forest and just kept shooting film, sooner or later I'd get something." She gave a heavy sigh. "I still can't believe I'm this close and I'm not even going to see the place."

I was about to head onto the highway that went to Frederick, but instead I pulled off the road. I don't know why I opened my mouth, but I did. "We could take the back road to Frederick," I offered. "It goes through Black Hills Forest. That way you could at least see the area."

"You mean it?" she asked, as if I'd just told her she'd won the lottery.

"Sure. It's no biggie."

"Cade." She sounded hesitant. "I'm going to ask you a favor, and I'll totally understand if you say no. But do you think we could actually go into the woods? Stop, I mean, on the way to Frederick?"

I didn't answer. I've been in Black Hills Forest many times, but it's not a place I hike casually.

"It's just that I've been waiting forever to see this,

13

and"—Laura glanced up at the sky, which was cloudless—"the afternoon light is pretty good. I think I could get some great pictures."

For a few seconds Laura reminded me of my cousin Heather. Intense. Focused. Driven. Determined to get to her goal.

"Well, I don't know how much time I have, but . . ." I checked my watch. We had time. We could take a detour, hike into the woods, and still get out of there before dark.

"Okay." I nodded and headed for the back roads. I figured it was actually a good choice, since the Morris Minor doesn't go more than forty-five miles an hour. Attempting to cruise the highways can be kind of embarrassing.

Laura gazed out the window intently, taking in the landscape as it changed from small, dingy roadside businesses and small houses to winding roads and total woods.

"Is this your first time back?" I asked, remembering that she'd said she was born around here somewhere.

Laura nodded. "Yeah, my parents moved to Minnesota when I was two."

"Why'd they move?" I asked.

She shrugged. "I have no idea. They never want to talk about it." She shrugged again. "Who knows? Parents."

Yeah, I thought. Mine were kind of weird sometimes, too. My dad's an engineer for a high-tech wireless company. When he's not at work, he's totally obsessed with fly-fishing. My mom went to law school, but she's never practiced. She sells health-food supplements to all her friends. Neither of them are home much. And they're not real happy that I spend so much time working on these case files. They want me to "get over it."

"How far?" Laura asked impatiently. "Are we almost there?"

"Not really," I said. "Sorry."

She drummed her hands on her knees. "You know, I've dreamed about these woods my whole life," she muttered softly, staring hard at the scenery.

"Really?" I said.

"You ever have recurring dreams?" she asked. "It's as if there's something in them you've got to find. Something they're trying to show you. That's how I feel about these woods."

She nodded and shot me a strange glance. Almost as if she'd said too much.

I felt an odd sense of excitement right then. This girl had some kind of energy that made me feel as if I were about to begin a real adventure. Maybe it was the way she stared out the window, as though she couldn't stand to wait five more minutes for the excitement to start.

I suppose I should have wondered about her

saying she'd dreamed of these woods all her life and that she had to find something in them. But I was too busy looking at her blond hair blowing in the wind and wondering if she had a boyfriend.

I pulled off the road near the trail. The second we came to a stop, Laura bolted out of the car.

"Hey, wait!"

She stopped and turned. "What? Am I going the wrong way?"

"I just want to be sure we take the right trails," I said. "So we don't get lost."

I had hiked the route to the exact spot where Heather's camera and film were found so many times that I knew the way by heart. In fact, I'd found a shorter trail. I could get in and out of the woods in under five hours if I didn't make any wrong turns. But only if I went *my* way and caught all the key landmarks.

"Let me go first," I said.

"Okay," Laura said. But we *are* going to Rustin Parr's house, right?"

"Yeah. That's what you want, isn't it?"

Her eyes turned serious as she nodded.

"But you know there's nothing there," I reminded her. "Just the ruins, since his house burned down. It's just the foundation, really—nothing more."

"I know," she said, but she sounded kind of disappointed.

16

As we walked, she asked me a million questions. I filled her in on a few obscure facts, but basically she knew the whole story forward and backward.

In the early forties, eight children disappeared from Burkittsville, one by one. The first was Emily Hollands, a sweet-looking little girl with long blond braids and glassy green eyes. Seven other kids were abducted shortly thereafter, over a period of several months. Finally in May of '41, a hermit named Rustin Parr, who lived in the woods most of the year, walked into a local market and said, "I'm finally finished."

To the horror of the townspeople, Parr confessed to murdering the missing children. All but one. He made the oldest boy, Kyle Brody, stand in the corner in the basement while he murdered the others. Kyle escaped but killed himself when he was twenty-one.

The police arrested Parr and then sent a search party into the woods, to his house. What they found there was unspeakable.

Later Parr calmly admitted to it all, saying he had tortured and killed his young victims for "an old woman ghost" who lived in the woods near his house.

And that was about it. Parr's house burned to the ground two months after he was hanged for the murders—but no one ever found out who set the fire.

"I dream about that house, too," Laura finally said quietly.

We were about halfway in by now, just passing

one of my landmarks—a fallen log with a big scorched mark where lightning had struck the tree. I had to pay attention here, or I'd blow it and take the wrong turn. So I was only half-listening.

"I dream about that part of the movie, where they're running through the house," Laura went on. "You know, at the end? And then I read about how that investigator found out it's Rustin Parr's house. The same house."

"But, logically, it can't be," I reminded her as we headed up a hill. "His house burned down in 1941, like I said."

"I know, I know. It's so weird. But you put that house picture on your Web site. So it had to be the same house."

NOTE FROM CADE MERRILL: *Laura meant the photo that accompanied an article on Kyle Brody, published twenty-five years after his disappearance. It showed a wall in Parr's house, covered with small handprints. And strange hieroglyphics that looked as if they were written in blood.*

It still gives me a jolt to look at that picture.

Because it was the exact same wall as in Heather's film. And the same writing.

I turned to look at Laura. She wasn't listening to me. She kept glancing from side to side, as if some kind of internal radar had suddenly kicked in. She picked up her camera and clicked off a shot of the woods.

"We're near, aren't we?" she said. "I can feel it."

I glanced at the ground, searching for another familiar landmark. Then I saw it: a huge boulder, with a V-shaped crack in it.

That told me that the house site—or what remained of it, anyway—was at the crest of the next hill.

Laura hurried past me, obviously unwilling to wait. But she twirled around joyously first, flinging her arms open wide.

"Thank you! Thank you forever for bringing me here!" she said, as if I'd taken her to Paris or something.

Then she ran ahead a few more feet, to the top of the hill, and stopped dead.

"Cade!" she called out. "I thought you said it was gone!"

I jogged to catch up with her.

"What?"

Laura's face was clouded. She was standing perfectly still, her arms clamped to her sides.

"The house," she whispered. "You said it burned to the ground."

I followed her gaze. She was staring at the ruined foundation where Parr's house used to be.

"Yeah. It did."

Her head snapped back toward me. "Then what's that?" she demanded, pointing.

What was what? It was the old, ruined house foundation. Nothing more. I shrugged again.

"The ruins," I answered.

Laura's eyes opened wide. "You don't see the house?" Her voice was thin, terrified. "I do."

2

I looked at Laura, startled and confused. Was she playing some kind of weird game? *Of course* I didn't see the house. It wasn't there.

She swallowed hard, lifted her camera, and started clicking away. She took tons of pictures, not just of the old house foundation, but of the trees. The woods. The ground littered with dead leaves and twigs. The clouds in the sky. The rocks.

Whoa. She's burning an awful lot of film on . . . nothing.

My head started spinning. What's going on here? I wondered. Is Laura nuts?

Or was Laura Morely *really* seeing something that wasn't there?

She wouldn't stop taking pictures. She was breathing heavily, as if she was fighting for each breath.

She shot every angle. The view to the east. The north. The west. The south. Then she took a close-up of the house's foundation. A medium shot. A long shot.

The more pictures Laura took, the faster she clicked away. She burned thirty-six shots in less than five minutes, then knelt in the leaves to change film. Her hands were shaking. Her hair was wet with sweat. Her smile was gone.

"You're going to shoot, um, *more*?" I asked in surprise.

She didn't look up. She just kept shooting. Again she reminded me of my cousin Heather. Intense. Focused. Driven.

Ten minutes later she had used up her second roll of film—another thirty-six.

Then she turned her back on the house and dropped to her knees again. She seemed exhausted.

Finally she took the exposed roll of film out of her camera and raised her face to me, like a small child.

"Cade, can we stop at a darkroom on the way to the bus station?" she asked. "I can't wait to have these developed."

"Uh . . . I think there's a twenty-four-hour photo place once we get into Frederick, but nothing faster."

"I don't use those instant places," she told me. "I'm shooting black and white, and I *always* develop my own film."

Laura suddenly stood up and headed down the trail—fast, as if she was trying to escape. I had to jump over some rocks and walk fast to keep up with her.

"Wait up!" I called.

She slowed down but kept her back to me.

"So, if you have to print all the pictures yourself, are you going to wait till you go home to Minnesota to develop the film?" I asked.

"I guess I have to," she said. "Unless you want to see them. I mean, I took all these pictures of the house."

The funny thing was, the minute she said it I realized I did want to see her photos.

Pictures of the house?

She caught the expression on my face and sighed. "Look, I know it sounds weird, but I *saw* it. I swear."

"Okay." I was willing to give her that much. "But *I* didn't. What makes you think it's on the film?"

"Who knows?" she muttered. "It's worth a try." Then she suddenly started looking around. "Where are we now, anyway? Was this where they brought Elly Kedward?"

"When?"

23

"When she was banished," Laura said. "In the 1700s."

"I don't know," I answered. "There are no real records from the town of Blair. The town was abandoned, and all the people who left made a pact to keep silent about what happened."

"Do you think she's still here now?" Laura asked, peering at me. "I mean, your whole Web site is so . . . I don't know. Scientific. It's like you're just gathering evidence, not taking sides. What do you actually *believe*?"

"I believe things have happened," I answered.

That was the best way I could put it.

Things *had* happened.

Things that couldn't be explained.

Laura was still looking at me, waiting.

"And I believe in the evil," I added quietly. "The evil that got to Heather."

That was something I rarely said out loud. I didn't even like to think about it. But it was true.

Laura didn't speak for the next hour. We hiked in silence, which was fine with me. But the farther we got from the Parr site, the more she seemed to relax. The tension began to leave her face, her shoulders.

Finally she said, "I really need to print this film."

I thought about it. For an instant a warning thumped in my chest—the kind of feeling you get

24

when you're on an empty street late at night and you're sure some shadowy person is walking behind you.

Then I said, "Well, our school runs an arts program during the summer. I think some classes meet on Saturday. I'm tight with Mr. Mellon, the photography teacher. I'll see what I can do."

"You mean he'll let us use the darkroom?" Laura's energy was back now. She seemed totally focused again.

"Probably. But I don't know if I can still reach him tonight. I may have to ask him tomorrow," I told her.

"I won't be here tomorrow," she said.

And that's when I opened the door for everything that followed. I totally ignored scientific detachment and all the little danger signs that had been flaring ever since Laura saw Black Hills Forest.

"Look," I said, "my folks are away. You could crash in our basement, if you don't mind sleeping on a cot. And getting a close-up view of my dad's fishing tackle."

"Mind? That would be perfect! But call your photography teacher tonight, okay?" she begged.

I laughed. I could tell she wasn't very surprised that she'd wound up with a place to stay. I had the feeling that Laura was used to getting her way. But I didn't mind. Laura was interesting. Intense, focused, but also fun. And I did want to see those pictures.

"Okay," I agreed. "I'll call him tonight."

"Great," she said, sounding relieved. "Then you'll see what I was talking about. You'll see the house—and everything else."

"Else? What else?" I asked.

But Laura wouldn't answer me. "Just wait," she said.

3

I turned the Morris Minor onto my street and braked hard. One of the Willoughbys' four-year-old twins was chasing a ball into the street. I waited until his mother caught him, grabbed the ball, and led him safely back onto their lawn. Mrs. Willoughby waved to me.

"Who's that?" Laura asked.

"My neighbor, Angela Willoughby. And either Max or Evan. I have trouble telling the twins apart. No wait, Angela always dresses Evan in green, so that was Max."

"I don't even know the names of the kids in my neighborhood."

"Well, I used to baby-sit for these guys when they were toddlers," I said.

"Ugh." Laura winced. "I can't stand being around little kids. Last summer I had a choice between being a camp counselor and working for the city dump. I chose the dump." She gave me a suspicious look. "You don't have any little brothers or sisters, do you?"

"None. I'm an only child."

"Me too," she said.

We went into the house, and she immediately started scanning the bookshelves. "That's weird," she said. "I expected you'd have all sorts of books on the occult and witchcraft."

"Those books are all upstairs in my room," I explained.

I showed her the basement, where I set up a cot for her, right next to my dad's fishing-tackle display case. Even though the basement was finished off, it wasn't too cozy down there. Grass-green indoor-outdoor carpeting. Bare white walls. A few old rattan chairs. A Ping-Pong table we never used.

It was just one big, open space. But at least there was a bathroom, so she could have some privacy.

"I'll order pizza," I offered. "What kind of toppings do you want?"

"Oh, I eat anything. But I'm beat," she answered. "I think I'll just crash. Do you mind?"

"Uh, no," I said. But for some reason I felt a little disappointed.

"See you tomorrow," she called as I headed up the stairs. "Don't forget to call your teacher."

"Yeah," I said. "See you."

〰

THE NEXT MORNING I woke up feeling that someone was watching me. I opened my eyes and found Laura standing over my bed. I sat up with a jerk.

"Is the high school open yet?" she asked.

I glanced at my alarm clock. Eight A.M.

"No," I said.

Laura wore jeans and a cropped gray athletic T-shirt. I blinked, suddenly aware that my hair always sticks up at weird angles when I wake up.

"Well, when does it open?"

I blinked again and tried to flatten down my hair without looking like an idiot. I spend most of my days staring at a computer screen. I'm not exactly used to having beautiful girls show up in my bedroom before I'm awake.

"Not until nine on Saturdays."

She grinned. "Hey, sorry. I just can't wait to see what's on the film."

"Yeah, okay," I said. "But I've got to shower first. And eat. You must be starving, too."

"Not really," she answered, shrugging. "I'm too

psyched. I can't wait to get into the darkroom." She tugged playfully at my covers. "Come on—out of bed, sleepyhead! What kind of witch-hunter are you, anyway?"

"Would you mind giving me a little privacy?" I grumbled, glancing toward the door.

"Oh, sorry. Okay. I'll give you ten minutes. But if you're not downstairs by then, I'm coming back."

I rolled my eyes. Great.

But I have to admit, I was pretty excited about seeing that film. And it wasn't that terrible waking up to see an exciting girl like Laura in my room.

I was dressed in five minutes and met Laura in the kitchen.

I gulped a cup of coffee and wolfed down two bowls of cereal.

Laura ate nothing.

I tried not to say anything, but I couldn't help wondering what she was living on. She hadn't eaten for almost twenty-four hours, as far as I could tell. But Laura didn't look as if she were starving. She had a great body.

I tried not to stare at her pierced navel, which was showing just below the cropped T-shirt. After all, my relationship with Laura Morely was strictly business. But a guy can dream, right?

We climbed into the Morris Minor and drove to school. The place was deserted. Regular classes had been out for a week. And the photography program hadn't started yet, but Mr. Mellon had left a key for me with the janitor, Mr. Regis, so we could let ourselves into the darkroom.

Laura got straight to work. It only took her thirty minutes to develop the film.

My heart was hammering as I waited for her to pull it out of the developing tank.

Was Rustin Parr's house really going to show up?

We both pushed in closer, staring at the film as she hung it up to dry.

I'm not a pro at deciphering negatives, but I didn't spot a house on any of the shots. They all looked like a bunch of rocks and trees to me.

"See anything?" I asked.

She shook her head, disappointed. "No. But I'm going to print them anyway."

"How long will that take?" I asked.

Laura sighed. "The film has to hang for a while, Cade." I felt kind of stupid until she suddenly grabbed me by the arm and pulled me toward the door. "I'm starved," she announced.

Finally, I thought. She eats. She's actually human.

We drove to a McDonald's, and I watched as Laura bolted down two Egg McMuffins, two hash browns, a large OJ, and hot tea with milk.

In between bites she grilled me about my life: friends, classes, school.

"Chemistry?" she said, making a face when I told her that was my favorite class. "I didn't figure you for a science geek."

I shrugged. So I didn't look like a science geek. Was that supposed to be a compliment?

Laura swirled the stirrer around in her tea. "Being into science, that's weird, with your interest in a witch legend."

"Actually, it's not weird at all," I said. "The Blair Witch story is a problem, a total mystery. And I'm looking for answers. It doesn't add up now, but I believe it will. The answers are out there, and the only way to find them is to look for them systematically."

"I guess so," Laura said, glancing at her watch.

We still had time, though. And I wanted her to understand. "Do you know what the single greatest scientific discovery ever made was?"

"I don't know—gravity? I don't know," she answered.

"No one does. Because there is no such thing as a *single* discovery. Every discovery comes as one of three or four or a hundred others all building together.

"That's what my site is about—collecting and analyzing all the little discoveries until it adds up to a big answer."

Laura stared at me the whole time I was talking, and then she did something that took me by surprise. She nodded and touched the back of my wrist. It was just a light touch, but at that moment she and I made a connection. I knew it. She knew it. But neither of us knew where the connection would take us. Neither of us said anything for what seemed like a long time. Then Laura jumped up.

"Oh, wow!" she exclaimed as she pointed to her watch. "The film should be dry. Let's go."

When we returned to the darkroom, I watched as Laura worked silently in the strange amber light that is safe for photographic paper. Moving from left to right, she filled four plastic trays with chemicals. The first one held developer. The second contained stop bath—to "stop" the development process. The third was something called fixer, to make the prints stable, or permanent. The fourth tray held plain water, to wash the other chemicals out of the prints.

Laura cut her negatives into strips and studied them. Again, there was nothing too interesting about them, as far as I could see. Just a lot of shots of trees and rocks, and the old stone house foundation.

She picked one of those—a shot of the Parr house foundation, where Heather's knapsack had been found. In my opinion, it was one of the least interesting shots she had taken.

Laura slipped it into the enlarger.

"How long does this part take?" I asked.

"Less than a minute," she said.

A moment later she exposed the image on a blank 8-by-10-inch sheet of photographic paper.

She carried it over to the tray of developer and slipped it in. I peered over her shoulder.

In less than fifteen seconds the image began to appear.

I sucked in my breath. Beside me I felt Laura freeze.

"Oh, my god," she muttered. "See?"

My heart was hammering in my chest. I couldn't believe it. Even in the amber light, we could see the image clearly.

It was a picture of a house—a whole house, not just the stone foundation. Laura was right!

But that wasn't the strangest part. Posed in front of the house were four people.

"Do you see them?" Laura said, her voice trembling slightly.

I studied the photograph. The people.

A man and a woman stood on the porch. From the clothing and hairstyles, the picture seemed to have been taken sometime around 1910. In front of the man and woman were twin boys, almost seven years old.

There was only one conclusion to be drawn.

Laura knew it and I knew it.

4

"One of those boys is Rustin Parr," Laura whispered, her voice sounding choked. "Right?"

I nodded, not quite able to speak myself.

It was. It had to be.

Rustin Parr and his twin brother, Dale.

I mean, I couldn't be positive. I had never seen a photograph of Rustin as a child. But I *had* seen pictures of his father, Wilson Parr. It was hard to be sure, but the man in the photo did look just like him.

"You see?" Laura said. "I told you."

"Is that what you meant?" I asked, staring into her eyes. "When you said 'everything else.' Did you see these people yesterday? In the woods?"

Laura's face was twisted, confused. "I don't know," she said finally. "I—I *felt* them there, I guess."

Suddenly she raced back to the enlarger and grabbed the negative carrier out of its slot. She held it up to the amber light, staring hard.

"There's nothing," she said finally. "Nothing on the negative except the stone foundation."

"What now?" I asked.

"We print another one," Laura said.

She pointed to frame number 7—a close-up of the stones.

But she could barely get the negative back into the holder, her hands were shaking so much.

My pulse must have been about 120.

It was tough to be totally rational. Part of me knew that this was really happening. It had the feel of truth—no matter how unreasonable that was.

I searched for a rational explanation. Was this some sort of trick? Maybe Laura had set everything up. She could have posed a bunch of people in old-fashioned clothes. Though if she had, why weren't they on the film?

If it *was* a hoax, it was unbelievably elaborate. I ruled out the possibility of there already being an image on the photographic paper. I had seen Laura open that package of photographic paper. There was no way she could have manipulated it ahead of time. The seal was unbroken.

Laura shook her hands in the air, to get them to stop trembling. Then she took a deep breath and tried once again to focus the image on the board.

I stared at the picture. It was a black-and-white reversal of how it would look when it was developed, but I could still see all the details plainly. There were no people and no house—just a close-up of the stone foundation.

Laura exposed the paper and then raced back to the developing tray. The first print was still there, with two childish faces staring up at us from beneath the liquid.

Laura slipped the second print into the chemicals and rocked the tray back and forth.

"I can't believe this is happening," she muttered.

Within seconds the image on the second picture appeared. This time the photo revealed a close-up of the twin boys—but with much more detail.

Horrible detail.

Although they were clearly twins, the boy on the left was handsome. He had an innocent face and a beguiling smile, as if he knew he could get whatever he wanted out of anyone.

The boy on the right, however, was strange looking. He made me think of a phrase my grandmother used to say. "He's not right." His features weren't ugly, but there was something about his expression that was definitely disturbing. His eyes were too wide open, as if he was shocked and terrified by the camera. And his grin was more like a sneer—a sinister sneer.

"Oh, my god," Laura gulped.

For an instant, she swayed on her feet. I reached out to touch her arm.

"Are you okay?" I asked.

"No." Laura shook her head. "I'm . . . totally freaked out. I think I'm going to puke."

"Maybe you'd better go sit down."

I glanced around for a chair, but I didn't see one in the eerily lit darkroom.

"I'll be okay," Laura insisted, but she gripped the sides of the sink for balance.

"You want to go outside? Get some fresh air?" I asked.

"I'm all right," Laura said. She lifted the second print out of the developer and held it a little closer to the safelight. "Which one do you think is Rustin?"

"I don't know," I said. "Hard to tell. Neither of them really looks like him as a grown man. But there's footage of him after his trial, right before he was hanged. He didn't have those strange eyes."

"They're . . . so cold," she said with a shudder.

"Can we get those prints dry and look at them out in the light?" I asked.

"Sure," Laura answered. She turned back to the deep sink that held the four trays. Then she lifted up both prints, let them drip for a moment, and slipped them into the second tray of chemicals.

The minute the prints hit the stop bath, they began to change.

"Oh, no!" Laura cried.

Like magic, the images had reverted to the boring scenes that were on Laura's negatives—the empty stone foundation, the dirt, the trees.

The twin images of Rustin and Dale Parr had completely disappeared.

5

"What happened?" I asked. "Do the prints usually change when you put them in that solution?"

Laura looked at me as if I were an idiot. "Are you kidding? The prints are supposed to *stop* changing when you take them out of the developer and put them in the other trays."

Laura lifted both prints out of the stop bath and tossed them angrily into the wastebasket.

Then she rinsed her hands and slapped them on her jeans to dry them.

"Why don't we try printing them again?" I suggested.

"That's what I'm doing." Laura bent over the enlarger to refocus the same negative, and went through all the steps again.

We both leaned in close over the developing tray to see what would come up.

"There they are," she whispered. She shot me a quick, excited glance.

I nodded.

The young twin boys stared up at us from the developer again. The one on the left was cherubic.

But the one on the right seemed even more sinister this time around.

"That one has to be Rustin," Laura said, pointing to the one on the right.

"Maybe," I said slowly. It made sense, since Rustin Parr grew up to become a deranged serial killer.

And yet . . .

"Well, here goes nothing," Laura said. She lifted the print out of the developer and dropped it into the stop bath.

The image of the twins disappeared.

Laura cursed under her breath.

"That's impossible!" I practically shouted.

Laura turned back to the enlarger again. Without saying a word, she immediately printed another negative.

We bent over the developing tray and watched.

"Who is that?" Laura whispered.

I shook my head and shrugged. This was so weird.

We were staring at another picture of Parr's house, but from the side, not the front. A woman stood in a window, waving. But it wasn't a friendly wave. She seemed to be gesturing to the photographer to go away.

"Must be the mother," I said. "It's the same woman from the first picture."

Laura went back to the enlarger and changed to another negative.

This time, when the image came up, we saw the two boys wrestling viciously in the front yard. Their mother stood near the front door, calling to them. She seemed to be scolding them, yelling for them to stop.

"Look, the sweet one's on top," Laura whispered. I could feel her breathing hard beside me. She was hyperventilating.

I leaned in closer.

"See?" Laura pointed to the two boys. "The angelic kid is beating the crap out of his brother. The one with the weird eyes is on the bottom. He's losing the fight."

"Let's print as many of these as we can," I said. "To see what else develops."

Laura ignored my stupid pun. She was all business. Over the next few hours she printed ten more negatives. Some of the pictures were ordinary shots of a house, curtains blowing in an open window. But others revealed strange, twisted scenes of family life—scenes we were never meant to witness.

Or were we?

In one the father was slaughtering a chicken, presumably for the family dinner, with the two boys observing. The sweet kid was laughing, but the weird kid cringed, hiding his eyes.

And this was bizarre. Although Laura hadn't actually stepped inside the foundation of the house, another photo revealed an interior shot of the parents' bedroom. The bed was unmade, and there was a deep depression in the mattress, as if a body had been lying there for a very long time.

The strangest photo contained just a ghostly blur, as if someone had been running across the frame when the shutter was clicked.

But each time Laura transferred the pictures to the stop bath, the eerie images disappeared.

I looked at my watch. We'd been in the darkroom all day, I realized. The school would be locked up soon.

"We've got to go," I said.

Laura ignored me and stuck another negative into the carrier.

"Hey, we don't want to be locked in here all night."

"We don't?" She shot me one of those flirty smiles.

I didn't answer.

"Just one more," she promised. She brushed a clump of blond hair out of her face and grabbed the negatives again. She scanned the shots, and finally she settled on the first one she had taken in the woods, before we even reached Rustin Parr's house.

The negative itself showed a single tree, an old oak.

But when it came up in the developer, we both gasped.

The initials *E.K.* were carved into the tree trunk.

Elly Kedward.

The Blair Witch.

The letters seemed to glow like a beacon in the dull amber light of the darkroom.

"No," I said, answering Laura's question before she could ask it. "That wasn't there before. I'm positive. I've walked those woods a million times. I'd have seen it. Hey, it's probably some kids playing a joke. Anyone could have carved that there."

Laura sighed and closed her eyes. Her shoulders sagged. She looked really wiped.

Finally she went back to the sink and lifted the print out of the developer. She was about to drop it into the stop bath when I grabbed her wrist.

"Wait. What happens if you don't put it in those other chemicals?" I asked. "Can we take it out of the darkroom and look at it?"

She shook her head. "I did it once. The image won't last, it turns black after a while."

"But at least for a few minutes, we could see it in the daylight?"

She nodded.

"Let's do it, then," I said. "We can show Mr. Regis—so we'll have another witness."

"Okay."

Laura laid the print faceup in an empty tray and headed to the darkroom door.

But by the time the two of us stepped into the hall, blinked from the brightness, and stared down at the tray in Laura's hands, the image was gone.

All that remained in the tray was a wet, white sheet of photographic paper.

"What happened?" I asked.

"I don't have a clue," she whispered. "It's just gone."

I didn't know what to think. Either Laura was pulling some kind of fast one on me, or . . .

. . . The secret of Rustin Parr was waiting for us back in the darkroom.

PART II:

Laura's Visions

Based on the journal of Laura Morely
and the notes and observations of Cade Merrill

6

NOTE FROM CADE MERRILL: *After the scene in the darkroom, the subject of Laura going right home to Minnesota just didn't come up. She came back to my place and wound up staying there until . . . until it was over.*

What follows is what happened in those next few days. You will notice that I have described events where I wasn't present. Those events I've reconstructed both from what Laura told me and from what I discovered later in her journal. For clarity's sake, I've chosen to relate the events in the order they happened—not in the order that I discovered them.

Laura woke up very early the morning after she developed the pictures, feeling starved.

No, just caffeine-deprived.

Tea, she thought. I've got to have my cup of tea.

She dug out a teabag from her pack and padded up the stairs to the kitchen to put the kettle on.

Unlike most of her friends from home, who were major night owls, Laura loved getting up in the morning. The earlier, the better. It was the only time of day when she didn't feel rushed and pressured to get things done.

She stirred some milk and sugar into her cup and thought about what had happened over the past two days.

What happened in those woods, anyway?

She shuddered, remembering. It was too much like the terrifying dreams she always had, ever since she could remember.

Dreams of the woods.

The house.

And more.

Things she didn't want to think about now. Or ever again, for that matter.

Did she really see a house that had burned down more than sixty years ago? Or did she simply dream it again? Imagine it?

One thing she knew for sure: The photographs were real. Cade had seen them, too.

I shouldn't have come back to Maryland, Laura thought. This trip was a mistake.

But she knew she was just kidding herself. There was no sense even thinking that way.

She had no choice. The dreams had been plaguing her for way too long. She *had* to come to Burkittsville—to find out what those woods were all about.

She glanced at the clock. There was no use hanging around here till Cade got up. It was Sunday, anyway, so they couldn't get back into the darkroom. The school was locked up.

She'd have to wait till Monday for another try.

In the meantime, she had to go back to those woods—and she had to go alone. Whatever was there, she knew it wasn't going to present itself to her if she had someone else tagging along.

Laura dressed hurriedly in layers, warm enough for the chill morning air, but with clothes she could shed as the day grew warmer. She slipped out of the house and hiked the two miles through town, toward the trail, her camera slung over her shoulder. She only stopped once to fill her backpack with bottled water and bags of trail mix.

"So where you headed?" the guy in the 7-Eleven asked, eyeing the water and munchies and her pack.

"Oh, I don't know," Laura told him vaguely. "Just

down the road, probably." *None of your business,* she added silently.

"Hey, you're not one of those Blair Witch groupies, are you?" He squinted at her. "This place has been crawling with them ever since those students disappeared and their movie came out."

Laura glanced up at the Blair Witch T-shirts they were selling behind the counter. She pretended to laugh.

"No way," she answered. "I'm a nature photographer." She gestured toward her camera. "I'm just trying to catch some pictures of ferns, flowers, leaves. That sort of stuff."

"Yeah?" The pimply young clerk raised one eyebrow. He obviously didn't believe her. "Well, you'll have to get a ways off the road for that. The only 'nature' on Route 17 is a bunch of dead skunks. You know, roadkill."

Someone behind Laura laughed. She whirled around and saw two guys in scuzzy black T-shirts and jeans, waiting to buy Gatorade.

"Thanks for the advice," she told the clerk, scooping up her change.

"Be careful in those woods," the clerk called after her.

"I'll remember that," she said on her way out the door.

Jerk.

In less than thirty minutes Laura was on the trail, the same one she and Cade had taken two days before. At least it *looked* like the same one. But was she really sure?

She hiked for another twenty minutes, scanning the landscape for something familiar. Anything.

This is dumb, she realized. And dangerous.

When Heather Donahue and her crew set out, they'd been carrying maps and a compass. And they still got lost.

What made Laura think she could just wander into Black Hills Forest, alone, and come out alive?

All at once, Laura's heart raced faster, jolted by the awareness that she was taking a huge, unreasonable risk. But she had no intention of turning back. She concentrated on the signposts, both natural and manmade, along the trails that she had walked two days before.

If she could remember Cade's shortcut, she'd be okay. But if she missed one turn . . .

"Emily!"

Laura froze.

Was that a voice?

She stood perfectly still, listening, the hairs on the back of her neck prickling.

"Where are you, Emily?"

Oh, my god, Laura thought, trying not to panic. Someone else is here in these woods. She couldn't tell whether the voice was male or female. Was someone following her?

Every muscle in her body told her not to move. Just hold still, she told herself. Don't give them a moving target. Don't show signs of fear. Don't . . .

Behind her, twigs snapped. She whirled around, but there was no one there.

A cold breeze brushed over her.

Stop it, Laura thought. There are lots of people in the woods. That's what the 7-Eleven guy said, right? Some kid's probably lost.

The breeze grew colder. Laura pulled her windbreaker tighter, her teeth chattering. What was going on?

"Help me!"

"Where are you, Emily? Come back!"

"I can't!"

Small, distant voices. Unreal voices. Children's voices, Laura realized, her throat tightening in fear.

Emily. Who was Emily?

Laura held still, listening hard.

Now there was sobbing. "Don't come here."

The little girl's voice, terrified, was warning her. Laura was sure of it.

She turned, slowly, just her shoulders at first. Then she looked behind her.

Nothing.

She peered hard into the woods, looking for movement.

Leaves on a branch fluttered in a breeze. That was it.

As quietly as she could, Laura kept turning, slowly, in a circle.

She had come up a small rise, so she had a good view down the hill.

Laura's breathing was shallow and fast, and her heart seemed to pound in her throat. Stay calm, she willed herself.

She waited. Two minutes. Three.

Nothing. The voices had stopped. The cold breeze was gone.

Okay, Laura thought. Maybe I imagined it.

Fine.

But she was still getting out of there—right now!

Don't run, Laura reminded herself. In case someone's watching. Don't let them know you're afraid.

She forced herself to move down the trail, slowly, back toward the road, though every muscle in her body said, "Danger. Get ready to run."

Her eyes darted right and left, checking the trail for landmarks. She didn't want to get lost now—not on her way back toward the road.

Finally she saw a boulder with a distinctive V-shaped crack.

Wait a minute, Laura thought. That was Cade's

last landmark—just before the hill leading up to Rustin Parr's house.

But it couldn't be! She'd only been hiking an hour. And she had turned back, away from the house.

She double-checked her watch.

Less than an hour.

There couldn't be two of those rocks. Could there?

She ran ahead, down the hill, and up another knoll. Then she stopped dead.

"Oh, my god," she said softly.

There it was. The old stone foundation, nothing else.

But the foundation can't be here, Laura thought. It's behind me. And much deeper into the woods. Hours away.

She glanced around quickly, checking for all the landmarks that she'd recorded in her memory, as well as on film. The clump of three trees to the east. The well-worn path that led to the ruins of the house. The stones at the base of . . .

Laura sucked in her breath.

What was *that*?

Near the base of the stone foundation lay two small clumps of sticks. At first they looked identical.

She took a few steps toward them and stopped.

The sticks had been carefully arranged in a pattern. Two patterns, really. One bundle was tied neatly together with a vine. The other was messy, crudely fastened together to form what seemed like some strange symbol.

Laura shuddered. These hadn't been here two days ago. Had someone placed these sticks as some kind of joke? Or was it a message for her?

For an instant she stood immobile, staring at the bundle, afraid to move any closer.

But she had to see them better.

She started forward, slowly reaching . . .

A loud scream tore through the silence.

"Get out of my yard!"

7

Laura jolted in terror at the sound of the voice. She whirled around.

It was a boy's voice, she was sure of it. A young boy, who clearly didn't want her here.

Unlike the other voices, this one sounded very near—no more than five feet away.

Laura drew her arms up to her chest, instinctively taking a defensive position. Waiting.

With all her heart she wanted to run away from this creepy place and out of the woods.

Pretend you're not here, she told herself. Be somewhere else.

But she *was* here.

And no matter how hard her heart was racing, she had to look at those sticks.

She took another step forward, then froze, listening for the voices again.

Silence.

Laura's throat felt tight.

Okay, I'm all right, she told herself. Nothing has happened. I'm not bleeding, I'm not being attacked, there's no one here to hurt me. It's a beautiful, warm July day, and I'm just hanging out in the woods, looking at some sticks that were probably put here by a bunch of local kids who think the whole Blair Witch thing is funny. They've probably played in these woods their whole lives. They're hiding in the trees somewhere right now, doing weird voices to spook me.

But in her heart Laura knew that wasn't true. She could sense that there was no one in the woods with her now. No one human, anyway.

Still breathing hard, she leaned closer to the bundle of sticks, holding her camera. The bundle was actually three sticks. One long one and then two branches coming out in a V. Was it an arrow? A *Y*? Or a person with arms raised? She focused, then clicked the shutter. Just once.

No, take a few more shots, she told herself. In case the first one doesn't come out.

Her body was casting a shadow, anyway. It would be better if she moved.

She glanced at the sun.

It would be better if I faced the other way, she thought. But then she would have to stand *inside* the outline of Rustin Parr's house.

Laura hesitated. For some reason, she had avoided stepping over the stone foundation the other day. And she still didn't want to.

If I step into the house, she thought, I'll actually be standing in the basement, where all those poor kids were tortured and killed.

Every instinct in her body told her not to do it.

Except one. From the moment Laura became serious about photography, she had trained herself to do anything—whatever it took—to get the right shot.

She stepped over the low stone wall—and her foot hit something hard in the dirt.

"Ouch," she said, annoyed. She kicked away some dried leaves and was astonished to see that she had stepped on an old movie camera, a heavy black metal one. It looked old-fashioned. Beside it lay several reels of film in rusty metal cans.

Laura's pulse raced.

Where did all this equipment come from? Did it belong to Heather Donahue?

No, Laura told herself. That's ridiculous. Heather

disappeared years ago, and this site has been searched many times since then.

Besides, she told herself as she carefully lifted the camera, this thing was too old. And heavy. No one in her right mind would lug around a camera as heavy as this!

Laura stood up and examined the camera, reading the thin metal label that was attached to the side with rivets. Victor Cine Camera, it said. Made in Davenport, Iowa.

On the side there was a small metal crank. Laura had seen a documentary about old movie cameras once. You turned the crank, then pushed the button to release a spring. When the spring was released, the film rolled.

The spring's probably dead, she thought, but she gave it a few cranks anyway. To her surprise, it was in good working order and moved easily.

Is there actually film in here? she wondered, putting the heavy camera up to her eye.

She pushed the release button.

At once there was a soft whirring sound as the film reel inside the camera began to spin.

Laura sucked in her breath and stared through the small, slightly stained viewfinder.

The images were very faint at first. But there was definitely something there.

This isn't possible, she thought. Film doesn't work this way. It isn't like video. You can't view it through the same camera you shoot it in.

All the rational facts spun through her head like a carnival ride.

But the most important fact remained.

She was actually seeing the film—what appeared to be old home movies. Laura immediately recognized the Parr family. The slightly faded images began to clear, revealing young Rustin and Dale, romping and fighting in the yard outside the house as their mother hung some washing on a clothesline.

Even more unbelievably, Laura could *hear* them. It should have been impossible—this was a silent film camera. No sound. But she could hear, very faintly, the boys talking, pleading, arguing, fighting.

This isn't happening, Laura thought, her throat growing tight again. This has to be another dream.

She tried to will herself to put the camera down. But she couldn't make herself do it.

Some powerful force was compelling her.

She couldn't let go.

She had to keep watching.

8

"You'll be sorry."

Rustin Parr's childish voice carried above the constant whir of the camera as the film continued to unwind. He was taunting his twin brother, Dale.

At least, Laura thought the mean-sounding boy was Rustin. She sensed it, somehow. But she couldn't be sure. Which boy was which? She thought of the twins who lived across from Cade—how one was always dressed in green so you could tell them apart. There was no such clue here.

The boys kept tumbling roughly on the lawn, not far from where Laura stood with the camera.

Let me stop watching now, Laura prayed. Let me drop the camera and run.

Her arms ached from holding the heavy camera up to her eye. But she was frozen to the spot, viewing the images and listening to the steady whirring.

Was she really watching the Parr family's home movies? Or was she actually *seeing* a vision of the boys? Her own private movies?

There was no way to tell.

A moment later the scene abruptly shifted.

Now the Parr twins' parents—Charity and Wilson—were standing together in a dark corner of the house, arguing.

"No!" Wilson Parr said harshly. "He's our son! We can't do that."

His wife twisted her hands, fear and worry creasing her brow. "But he's not normal," she whispered.

"Well, no one knows that," Wilson retorted sharply. "*You* don't even know that for sure, woman!"

"I've seen what he does to his brother," she answered, her voice small. "He nearly kills poor Dale, he does."

Then the scene shifted again, as if whoever had been holding the camera had suddenly stopped shooting.

The next segment of film was silent. The twin boys worked side by side, gathering sticks. Into bundles. Just like the ones she'd seen earlier. The strange-looking child's bundle was tied carefully, neatly. The sweet-looking child's bundle was gathered sloppily, sharp sticks jutting out in all directions, the vine rope twisted and frayed.

Laura shuddered.

To her relief, a few moments of blank film followed. But the camera was still whirring.

Then a new scene appeared. Now the two boys were in the front yard again. The sunny, unblemished boy sat astride his brother, pummeling him.

I've seen this image already, Laura thought suddenly. In the darkroom at Cade's school. I took a picture of that.

"Stop, Rustin, stop!" the child on the bottom cried.

"Rustin! Get off your brother!" the woman at the front door called.

The sweet-looking child didn't look at his mother.

"It's Dale's fault!" he whined. "He started it."

"Rustin Parr, you know very well Dale never starts anything," Mrs. Parr scolded. "Now let your brother go, and come help your pa with the fire."

"Aaahhh!" the boy on the bottom screamed as his laughing twin stood up and gave him one final, hard kick.

Then the film blurred and went blank again.

Laura felt dizzy. Her head was spinning as she tried to take everything in.

Rustin Parr was definitely the sweet-looking twin.

But he was the one with the evil nature. And Dale was the one with the weird eyes and the sneering grin. But he was the one with the innocent heart.

Finally the whirring stopped, and Laura nearly dropped the camera. Her hands ached from holding it so long—but she was free from its power at last.

"Dale! Come here, child. Are you all right?"

"Yes, Mama. I'm fine."

No! Laura told herself wildly. The "movies" weren't running anymore. The camera was completely turned off.

She dropped the camera to the ground, as if it had given her an electric shock, and ran blindly from the house, leaping over the stone foundation.

"Rustin, put down that stick!"

"Aw, Ma!"

Stop! Laura thought. I'm not hearing this!

She dashed toward the trees, unable to escape the voices. They were running through her head. They were part of her—and she couldn't escape them!

9

Laura's hands flew to her ears as she whirled away from the house, running from the voices.

This is a nightmare, she thought, closing her eyes tight. Worse than the dreams I had back home. I'm in some kind of nightmare—and it will never go away!

She wanted to scream and beat her fists on a nearby tree to make the voices stop.

But there was no escape.

I never should have come here, Laura thought.

She whirled desperately in circles, trying to spin so fast that she wouldn't hear the sounds. Then she fell to the ground, covering her ears with her hands.

Please, she prayed. Make it stop!

A moment later the voices slowly faded—and fell silent.

Laura had no idea how much time passed before she dared to move from the spot where she had fallen to the ground. It didn't matter.

All she knew was that she had to push away the images that danced on the edge of her consciousness.

When she finally opened her eyes, warm sunlight dappled the ground in front of her. A sparrow chirped in a distant tree, and a breeze blew softly.

The world was back to normal.

She hoped.

Slowly Laura turned her head and glanced back toward the clearing.

The house was gone. Only the stone foundation remained, just as it had for the past sixty years.

The heavy movie camera lay in the dirt, just inside the wall where she had dropped it.

I'm going nuts, Laura thought.

No.

It's worse than that.

Something is happening to me. Something I have no power to control.

She rose slowly to her feet, trying to breathe normally. With every ounce of strength she possessed, she willed herself not to look back again. But she couldn't help it.

She turned and glanced at the camera once again.

For an instant, Laura considered running down the trail, back to the road, and leaving it behind forever.

Some part of her desperately wanted to do that.

But that's not what I came here for, she told herself. I came to this place for answers.

Cautiously she crept up to the stone foundation and reached across it, lifting the camera and the cans of film out of the dirt.

She stuffed them into her backpack and swung it over her shoulders.

The heavy metal gear smacked her in the back, hard.

"Ouch." She tried to adjust the backpack, but no matter what she did, the camera jabbed her in the back, like a constant reminder that this whole experience was going to leave her painfully sore. Maybe bloody. And certainly bruised.

NOTE FROM CADE MERRILL: *Not much is known about Rustin and Dale Parr's childhood. But I can say that there is absolutely no record of it being a violent one. Nothing came out at the trial or after to indicate that Rustin and Dale had anything but a normal sibling relationship. Dale died when he was nine years old in a hunting accident.*

10

"Cade, you're finally awake," Laura said as she burst into the kitchen at about noon that day.

"Of course I'm awake," I snapped. "I've been up for hours waiting for you." I had to admit, I'd been sort of worried, getting up and finding her gone. No note or anything. "Where have you been, anyway?"

"To Rustin Parr's house," she said casually, leaning back against the refrigerator. She looked tired. Dead tired.

I glanced at the clock above the stove. No way. She could only have been gone about five hours, total.

Was I really supposed to believe that she'd hiked through town and that far into the woods and back in that amount of time?

"I know," Laura said, as if she had read my mind. "I can't explain it, either. I heard voices in the woods, and I started running back toward the road, and then all at once the house was just *there*—in front of me."

I frowned. What was she talking about?

She dragged herself into the family room, slung her heavy backpack onto the couch, and dropped down beside it.

I followed her.

Like I said, she looked exhausted. Her hair was sweaty, and her face and arms were covered with dirt. And the expression in her eyes—well, it's hard to describe. Kind of cloudy—and scared at the same time.

"I think I'm in over my head," Laura told me.

"What do you mean?" I asked, sitting down on the couch beside her.

She shrugged. "There's something out there, in those woods, and I'm—I don't know . . ." She searched for the right word. ". . . *connected* to it."

"Why do you think that?" I asked.

Laura was quiet for a moment. Then she reached into the backpack, pulled out the old camera and film, and told me what had happened. How she had seen those old movies, first through the camera, and then in her head. "I feel like I was led there," she finished. "So I could see those things."

"Why would someone want you to see them?" I asked.

She looked at me as if I were out of my mind. "How am I supposed to know?" she demanded. She started shaking. "It was horrible when I was seeing them without the camera. They got inside me somehow. I couldn't make them stop."

Had she been hallucinating? I had to allow for the possibility. In 1996 soil samples taken from the foundation of the Parr house showed evidence of opiates.

"Did you drink anything when you were near the house?" I asked.

"Not up there. I was too freaked. Earlier, though, I drank some bottled water I got at the 7-Eleven. Why?"

"Never mind." Even in Burkittsville bottled water is pretty reliable.

Laura rubbed her temples. Like she was trying to get rid of a massive headache. "I'm not sure who yelled at me to get out of his yard. It felt like one of the twins yelling at me." She gave me a look that reminded me of a trapped animal. "Do you think they could see *me*? Oh, god, what if they did?"

Her story didn't make much sense, but somehow, I believed her. I sensed a fear in her that couldn't have been faked.

I could feel my own excitement growing. This could be it. I was finally on the threshold of proving that there was some sort of supernatural occurrence in the Black Hills.

"Do you know anything about theories of time?" I asked her.

She gave me another one of those are-you-nuts? looks and shook her head no.

"We're used to thinking of time as linear," I explained. "Past followed by present followed by future. But there's a theory that says all times are parallel and ongoing. In other words, the past is still happening, just on another plane. So I'm wondering if it's possible that you were given glimpses into another plane of time."

"What if I was?" Laura sounded slightly hysterical.

I realized that was the wrong approach. "Okay," I said. "Forget that idea. Let's back up. I need you to try to remember as many details as you can. In the beginning, when you heard that voice warning you away, and then a voice calling Emily's name, was the voice male or female?"

"I don't know," Laura said in a dull tone. She wrapped her arms around herself. "Does it matter?"

"Yes," I told her. "Emily was the name of one of the seven children that Rustin Parr killed. So can you remember anything about the voice that spoke to her?"

Laura shut her eyes and put her hands over her ears. "I can, but I don't want to. I don't want to hear or see any of it again!" Her shoulders began to heave then, and she began to sob.

I stared at her, not knowing what to do. I'd been investigating the Blair Witch phenomenon for years. Now here in my living room was someone who might have more personal information than anyone I'd ever contacted. I wanted to shake the information out of her, getting every drop. But I could see she was in no shape to talk.

Laura sat slumped on the couch. She'd stopped crying, but she looked totally wiped out. The camera and reels of film lay at her feet.

"Have you looked at the film in those cans?" I asked her.

She shook her head and closed her eyes briefly. "I don't know if I want to see any of it," she admitted softly.

"We have to." I stared at her. "If it's really Rustin Parr's family's film, it would be an invaluable tool."

Then another, even more important thought occurred to me.

"It might even be more of Heather's footage," I said slowly.

"I didn't think of that," Laura answered. She looked at the floor. "I want to help you find out what happened to Heather," she said. "I really do, Cade. It's just that—well, you weren't there in the woods with me today. It was terrifying. I swear, it really felt like my life was in danger."

I reminded myself to stay detached, systematic, analytic. I couldn't abandon my own investigation. But I also couldn't help feeling sorry for Laura Morely. I was the only one who knew what she was going through. She needed someone to believe her. To be with her and help her. I was the only one who could help her.

"It'll be okay," I told her. I put on a phony deep voice and tried to sound like Batman or something. "I'll protect you, Laura Morely."

She gave me a tiny grin. "Shut up, Cade," she said.

I shrugged. "Hey, I was just trying to cheer you up. Come on, there's a projector at school."

I reached for the film cans.

"Closed," she reminded me. "Sunday."

"Right." Now it was my turn to fall back onto the couch in a slump.

"I don't mind waiting till tomorrow," Laura said, curling up against the pillows. "It's cool. Do you mind if I stay one more night?"

I didn't mind. There was no way I could think of sending Laura back to Minnesota. We were in far too deep by then.

As I watched, Laura's eyes closed and she drifted

off to sleep. She looked so innocent, lying there beside me.

After Laura fell asleep, I called Mr. Mellon and asked him to meet us at school the next morning. I didn't tell him the real story, just that a friend of mine had some reels of film she wanted a few opinions on. The truth was, I wanted an outside observer—someone objective—to see what was on the film Laura had found in the woods.

I also wanted him to be a witness when we printed Laura's negatives again, although I didn't mention any of that on the phone. It would have seemed too weird trying to explain it out loud. I already had something of a rep for dabbling in stuff that a lot of people thought was bull.

I figured we'd just go into the darkroom after viewing the Parr home movies and see if those images appeared again. And Mr. Mellon would be there to witness it.

We got to school at ten the next morning. After I introduced Laura to Mr. Mellon he unlocked the media storage room and wheeled one of the projectors into a classroom. As I popped the first reel onto the spindle, Laura pulled down the shades to darken the room.

"So Cade tells me you're a photographer," Mr. Mellon said, threading the projector as if he'd done it a million times in his sleep.

"Mm-hmm." Laura hopped up onto one of the desks.

"Documentary? Portraits? Landscapes? What's your specialty?" he asked.

"Landscapes," she answered flatly.

I glanced at Laura. For some reason, she was being pretty uncommunicative.

Mr. Mellon didn't seem to notice. "Okay, hit the lights," he told me.

I did, and he flipped the switch to start the projector rolling.

The film ran for a minute, just the blank clear leader at the beginning, with black scratch marks all over it.

"Come on," I muttered, eager for the images to appear.

But the film continued to roll on, exactly the same way—blank.

There was absolutely nothing on that film.

Mr. Mellon shifted uncomfortably.

"Too bad there's no fast forward," I said, trying to fill the awkward silence.

No one answered.

The three of us watched a full ten minutes of blank film, just staring at the screen, hoping something would show up near the end.

It didn't.

"Maybe the other reels aren't blank." Laura's voice was small.

"Let's hope so," Mr. Mellon said with a wry laugh.

Laura put the first reel back in its can and handed Mr. Mellon the second one. The reel itself was rusty, so Mr. Mellon had to bend it a little to get it onto the projector.

I hit the lights again.

The projector whirred.

Still nothing.

The last reel was empty, too.

The three of us sat in the dark room. Thin slanted bits of light filtered in from the edges of the window shades. Mr. Mellon looked at me questioningly. Laura was silent.

She hadn't said a word through most of this.

I couldn't read her mood. Was she mad at herself? Disappointed? Relieved? Did she feel embarrassed about showing my photography teacher three reels of blank film?

Or was she hiding something? Had she known this would happen?

She wouldn't meet my eyes, so I didn't know what to think.

Rationally I had to accept the possibility that the film had always been blank. That Laura had never seen anything in the woods. But when I tried to convince myself of that one, I couldn't. Maybe it was because there was something about Laura that was special. Maybe it was simply that she'd been so scared. But even though I knew the facts didn't support her story, for the first time ever I didn't care.

Mr. Mellon cleared his throat. "Well, I've got some work to do in my office," he announced, standing up. "And if my memory serves me correctly, you promised to help clean up the darkroom, didn't you, Cade? In exchange for using it the other day?"

I nodded. "Sure thing, Mr. Mellon."

"I guess you'd better get busy then," he said. "We can put away the projector later. Let's go downstairs, and I'll show you what needs to be done."

"Okay." I followed him out into the hall. Laura stayed behind.

When we were alone, Mr. Mellon turned to me, keeping his voice low, and said, "Can I ask you something, Cade?"

"Sure, what?" I said.

"How long have you known that girl?" he asked.

"Uh, not long," I admitted. "Just a few days, really. Why?"

He sort of shook his head. "I can't put my finger on it, but there's something about her that worries me. After eighteen years of teaching, you get a sense for when a kid's in trouble. Now, I don't know if she's using drugs or is going through difficult times at home, but something's eating at her."

I nodded as we walked down the echoing hallway. Something was eating at her, all right, but it wasn't what he thought.

Then I heard something that really gave me the creeps.

I looked back toward the classroom, where Laura still sat, alone.

The projector was whirring, its reels turning.

Laura was watching the films again.

PART III:

The Curse

Based on the testimony, written and
oral, of Laura Morely

11

They think I'm crazy. They think I'm a total flake, Laura told herself as she sat in the empty classroom.

They don't believe I saw those movies in the woods.

She sat there on the desktop, dangling her legs off the edge, feeling lonelier than she'd ever felt in her life.

Lonely and afraid.

Minnesota, home, her friends. They all seemed so far away now, like another lifetime. She'd left them behind. She felt totally alone—as though no one could follow where she was going now. But she knew.

She had to keep going. She *never* let herself give up. No matter how hard or frightening things became, she always toughed it out.

Laura glanced toward the windows. The dark green shades blocked out whole chunks of the world, large rectangles of darkness.

She hopped off the desk and started toward the windows to raise the shades and let in some light.

That was when she heard the movie projector behind her start to roll.

Startled, Laura whirled around.

Had Cade come back and turned it on?

No.

The projector was running all by itself—backward this time, the film rewinding slowly through the sprockets.

Only this time the film wasn't blank.

Laura walked closer to the screen, terrified and transfixed.

In fuzzy black and white the film showed a baby's room in a house somewhere. Not Rustin Parr's house, though. A newer one with cheerful teddy bear wallpaper. A woman walked into the nursery, carrying a baby about six months old.

For a few moments the film became too blurry to see.

But then it cleared a bit, and Laura saw that the

woman was wearing a University of Maryland sweatshirt and jeans.

Laura gasped.

The woman looked younger, of course—more like the photos in their albums at home. Her hair was longer then, and she was thinner. But there was no doubt in Laura's mind: The woman was her own mother!

And that means the baby is me! Laura realized. She peered even more closely at the screen, fascinated.

She watched as her mother hugged her, rocked her, changed her clothes, then placed her in her crib.

Laura thought her mother's face looked lined with worry as she bent down and mouthed the words "Good night."

Then she headed to the door, turned out the lights, and left.

But still, somehow, the film rolled on.

The camera began to pan the room, taking in a wider view. Then it moved in on the crib and the mobile hanging over it.

Laura gripped the nearest desk, unsteady. The mobile wasn't teddy bears or clowns. It was made of rough sticks. Sticks bound together to look like a human figure, the evil totem of the Blair Witch.

The stick doll dangled over the crib, twirling

slightly, suspended from somewhere higher, out of view.

Laura shivered, remembering the bundled sticks she'd found at the old Parr homesite.

The camera panned suddenly to the right and zoomed in on a stack of children's blocks in the corner on the floor. They were stacked in a strange, seemingly impossible formation. Two of the blocks were perched on their edges but didn't fall.

And instead of alphabet letters on the sides, there were odd symbols carved into each one.

Laura had seen those symbols before.

They were exactly like the odd letters written on the walls in Rustin Parr's house.

Laura edged toward the door, still watching the action on the screen behind her. She couldn't help it. She couldn't look away.

Silently, slowly, the camera moved back to the crib, to the child gazing innocently up at the stick doll hanging over her head.

The camera held there, focused on the baby.

On me, Laura thought.

The film was grainy, but even with the imperfections, she could see that there was something odd on the baby's forehead.

Laura squinted in the dark and forced herself to approach the screen.

There, on her own forehead, was a strange mark, a symbol of some sort.

Laura wanted to scream or look away. But she couldn't. She stared at the bloody red symbol that was carved deeply into the baby's skin.

12

"Nooo!"

Laura's scream sounded like the howl of an injured animal.

But no one heard her.

She was completely alone.

The projector stopped abruptly, and the tail of the film spun on its reel.

Laura felt a quick stab of relief. But the image of the marked baby—of herself as a marked child—terrified her.

She had no idea what that symbol meant. But she recognized it. It was the same shape as the bundle of sticks she had seen in the woods.

Was it some kind of curse? And who—or what—had placed it there?

The Blair Witch. It had to be. That was why Laura had found those sticks in the woods. She was meant to see that mark. It was *her* mark.

She was shaking.

Then her hand flew up to her forehead.

"I don't have a scar! That isn't me," she assured herself.

Trembling and frantic, Laura ran to the classroom door and gazed up and down the hall. Then she took a guess and raced to the nearest rest room.

She pushed into the cold tiled space, desperate to find a mirror. Still shaking, she ran to the sinks and pushed her shaggy blond bangs off her forehead.

Her reflection smiled back at her. It was a death-mask smile, strained and stretched.

But her huge feeling of relief was real.

There was no scar—her skin was smooth and un-blemished.

For the first time all morning, Laura began to breathe almost normally.

That baby wasn't me, she thought, heading slowly back toward the classroom. I don't have a scar. I don't have a scar.

Unless . . .

Laura stopped dead in the hallway.

A memory was coming back to her, something she hadn't thought about for years.

The accident!

Laura had almost forgotten. No one had talked about it for years. Her mind raced, remembering the details as she put it all together. The first time her mother had told her that story was when Laura was five. Laura's kindergarten teacher had read the class a book about a girl who went to the hospital.

Laura had come home and questioned her mother.

"Was I ever in a hospital?" she had asked. "I think I remember being in the hospital."

Her mother had looked startled.

"Why, yes, dear," she had said finally. "What do you remember about that?"

"The room. It had pink curtains," Laura had told her.

So her mother had told her the tractor story that day, for the very first time.

In her mother's story, Laura was eighteen months old—old enough to walk, but too young to remember. It happened just after her family moved from Maryland to Minnesota.

Her father had borrowed a tractor from a neighbor to mow the acreage they'd bought. Laura was riding with him when the tractor suddenly hit a rocky patch her father couldn't see. Laura was thrown clear and landed on a pile of jagged stones, which cut her forehead.

Luckily, her mother told her, they had found a plastic surgeon in Minneapolis who was able to remove the scar. Wasn't she a lucky girl?

Laura could hear her mother saying those words each time she told her the story.

Remove the scar. Lucky girl.

Laura had asked her mother why she didn't remember the accident, only the hospital.

"You were older. The scar was removed more than a year after the accident—when you were almost three."

That made sense. There was only one problem.

The story was a lie.

Her parents had taken her to a plastic surgeon, all right—to remove the witch's mark that had been placed on her as an infant!

Because it *was* a witch's mark, Laura thought. What else could it be?

Then another memory began to come back—or was it a dream?

There was a dark road near some thick woods. It was night.

She was a baby, too young to walk. Someone was holding her. But not her mother. Her mother was screaming for her.

"Laura! Laura!" And then, "For god's sake, give her back to me!"

She couldn't remember anything else. Not how she got there, or what happened next. But she clearly remembered the terror in her mother's voice. In fact, she could practically hear it right now.

Maybe that's when it happened, Laura thought.

Was that why her family had moved to Minnesota? To escape the witch's curse?

Laura shuddered. Was this why she'd been drawn, almost against her will, to return to Maryland?

Was this why her dreams were always so real?

There was only one way to find out.

She would have to return to the Black Hills Forest—and wait for a sign.

NOTE FROM CADE MERRILL: *Laura's suspicions, while unproven, are not entirely implausible. The legend of Elly Kedward contains numerous examples of her luring children and then bleeding them. Unlike other baby snatchers found in myth and folklore (the Biblical Lilith or Mexico's La Llorona), the Blair Witch sometimes allows the children she's taken to return to their families. Robin Weaver is probably the best-known example of this. And yet according to the legends, once the Blair Witch takes the children, they're forever changed. They somehow belong to her. Or are possessed by her. Is that what happened to Laura?*

13

Laura glanced at the clock on the classroom wall. Cade had been gone for nearly an hour, cleaning the darkroom. She could go find him. Or she could do what she was being called to do. She could return to the woods. To seek the answer.

Suddenly it seemed clear. All the power is in the woods, Laura thought. The power to overcome the curse is in the woods. That was why she had been drawn here. That was why she must go to the woods. Now.

Laura let herself out of the school building and started toward the forest. She had to face the evil. Running from it wouldn't help. But facing it was draining her.

She tried to push the thoughts of the witch and Rustin Parr away, but they were always there. The images flashed in her mind. The horrible movies were always playing in her head.

Rustin with a stick, hiding in some bushes. Pushing the stick out to trip Dale, gouging him in the leg.

Rustin setting an animal trap and covering it with leaves. Feigning an injury nearby. Calling his twin for help.

Rustin digging up worms and animal droppings. Mixing them into Dale's meat pie.

"Leave me alone!"

Laura's head spun. She was almost at the woods now.

With all her heart she wished that she could just go home.

Don't be here. Be somewhere else, she told herself, as she had every day since she'd come to Burkittsville—and every time she'd had one of those terrible dreams, ever since she was a little kid.

But that wasn't a choice anymore. She knew that. She trudged on to the woods. She couldn't stop now, any more than she could push the visions away.

The images rolled on, a jumble now—snippets of one moment, then the next. Some of the scenes seemed innocent. A family meal. Wilson Parr building a fire. Charity mending her dress.

But others made Laura want to close her eyes and never open them again.

Even if it meant that she was dead.

The evil smirk on young Rustin's face was too horrible to watch. She was on the path now, heading toward Rustin Parr's house.

"Dale! There's a surprise in your bed," Rustin called.

"Leave me alone!"

Was that her voice? Or was it young Dale's pleading with his brother to stop?

Laura crouched on the path, trying to shut out the voices. I want to go home, she thought. Home. I don't belong here.

But she did. She knew it.

"You boys bring back firewood now," Wilson Parr said sternly. The scene blurred, then changed again.

Rustin was hiding in the woods, a sharp rock in his hands.

Laura squeezed her eyes shut, even though she knew it was useless. Was this the vision she'd been dreading? Yes.

Masking a smile, Rustin called to his brother for help.

"Ow!" Rustin cried. "Dale! Help! I think a rattler bit me!"

Dale emerged from the bushes, his face clouded.

He seemed to know that this was probably a trick. Another trap. But if Rustin was hurt, he couldn't leave him. His brow furrowed with concern, he ran toward the sound of his twin's voice.

"Rustin, are you okay?" he called in a quivery tone. "Where are you, Rustin?"

Suddenly the image blurred. For once, Laura didn't see clearly at all. She breathed a sigh of relief.

Then there seemed to be a swift and terrible blow—and a thud as Dale's body slumped to the ground.

Laura's hands flew to her mouth to hold back the scream. Her body rocked back and forth.

No. No. No!

The images came rapidly after that: the symbols, the strange bloody writing, the picture of Dale lying in a shallow grave, with bundles of sticks bound to his face, wrists, arms.

And then there were screams—horrible, terrified screams. Children shrieking. Laura didn't know who or where.

Finally everything stopped. Is it over now? Laura wondered.

Slowly she opened her eyes. Was that my curse: to see Dale Parr's murder at the hand of his own twin brother?

A soft breeze brushed Laura's face. She gazed up toward the sky, hoping for some kind of answer. There was none. The day was cloudy but bright.

Laura squinted as she waited, listening. The woods were almost silent, with only the occasional sound of a squirrel running through the brush.

I'm free, she told herself, getting to her feet again.

But as soon as she began to move down the path, the hateful visions started once again.

This time the words were whispered, a hushed conversation between Charity and Wilson Parr in their bedroom.

All the curtains were drawn tight.

"No," Charity said. "He's still our son. We can't tell them the truth."

"But our other boy is dead!" Wilson said, his voice cracking and rising. "Do you understand that, woman?"

"That's *her* fault, not ours," his wife insisted.

Wilson buried his tormented face in his hands. "Who would believe that?" he muttered. "They'll lock us both up if we start talking that way."

Charity gripped her husband's wrists. "Now listen to me, Wilson. We'll say it was an accident—a hunting accident. That's all. No one will doubt us—not when we're talking about our own son. And the scar is gone."

Laura froze.

Scar?

Did Rustin Parr have a mark, too? Like the one she'd had? Was it part of the same curse?

Laura's head spun. The visions kept rolling, blending together, a hideous jumble of sights and sounds.

She started running toward the road, almost blindly. The images kept getting in the way.

She saw herself as a baby again, in her crib. The ugly scar was still visible on her forehead, and the stick doll dangled menacingly overhead.

But suddenly the vision swirled, the mind-camera panning around the room, past a second, empty crib.

A *second* crib?

Who was that for?

And then the camera moved to the walls. . . .

"No!" Laura screamed, stumbling as she ran. She tripped, falling on her face in the dirt, scraping her hands.

Once again she squeezed her eyes shut tightly, desperate to force away the awful vision.

But it was burned into her brain.

Tiny, bloody handprints danced across the walls of her childhood room, marching toward the ceiling in a border of blood!

NOTE FROM CADE MERRILL: *Twenty-five years after Parr's death a national magazine published a retrospective on the killings that featured photographs of Parr's house. One shows an inside wall covered with tiny bloody handprints. It's been* assumed that they were the prints of the children he killed. But there's no actual proof of that, nor is there anything that tells us if the prints belonged to one, two, or all seven of the children.

As to Laura's account of Dale's death, it runs contrary to the facts as they have been believed so far. Dale was killed while hunting with his father. Rustin wasn't with them. Or so they say.

PART IV:

The Family

*Based on the notes and recollections of Cade Merrill
and phone interviews with Ellen Morely*

14

When I heard that projector turn on, I was going to go back and see what Laura was up to. But by the time I finished cleaning the downstairs darkroom for Mr. Mellon and got back to the classroom, Laura had packed up the three reels of film and was out of there. I checked the parking lot, figuring she was hanging out in the Morris Minor, but no. She wasn't in the car.

Laura didn't show up at my house again until late that night. Like that morning, she was sweaty, and there was a big black smudge on her face.

"Where were you?" I asked.

"Walking." She sounded guarded, distant. "I

thought you'd be helping your teacher all day, so I went to get some air. I guess I lost track of time."

"I thought we were going to print your photos again," I said.

Her face softened for a second. "Oh, right. Sorry, I . . ." Her eyes begged me to understand. "I couldn't."

"Well, why not?" I was worried about her, but it came out sounding like I was irritated.

She shook her head, and the distant gaze returned. "I just couldn't," she said lamely.

"You went back to the woods?"

She shrugged. "It almost doesn't matter. No matter where I am, I keep seeing those movies in my head. Listen, no offense, but I don't feel like talking now."

I wasn't sure what to say to that. Grilling her with questions clearly wasn't going to work. I didn't want to make her any more upset than she already was. On the other hand, I wanted to see what was on that film.

Things were happening to Laura—things that I had actually witnessed, like her photographs of Rustin and Dale Parr. Those were amazing. It was breakthrough stuff—the closest I'd come to finding physical proof of supernatural phenomena in the Black Hills. And that's what I desperately needed.

"Well, can I have the negatives, then?" I asked. "Maybe I can get Mr. Mellon to help me print them."

Laura's face clouded. "I don't think so, Cade. . . ."

I threw up my hands, annoyed. "Look, Laura, we've got a problem," I said. "You don't want to tell me what you're up to, you don't want to print the pictures, and my parents are coming home tomorrow. I think they're going to be sort of surprised to find someone living in our basement. I'm not sure how much longer you can stay."

She looked at me with totally tired eyes. I was instantly sorry I'd snapped at her.

"You mean you want me to leave? *Now?*" she asked.

I shrugged. "No. Not really. I just want . . ."

Suddenly I wasn't sure what I wanted. Okay, I've always wanted things to make sense. That hadn't changed. But now I also found myself wanting to help Laura. And I was beginning to wonder if those things were in direct conflict.

I shook my head and walked out. Heading straight to my room, I got on the Internet and spent the rest of the night running searches for other photographic phenomena—without much luck—and I also started writing up the case file on what we had so far.

I guess I wouldn't have been so ticked off if I'd known then what had happened to her earlier that day in the classroom. Or if I'd admitted to myself that I was losing my detachment.

I don't believe you can see clearly if you're too

emotionally involved in a situation. I count on the fact that I approach the Blair Witch files with a certain scientific objectivity. Where Laura was concerned, that objectivity was evaporating faster than a drop of water in a desert. And that scared me.

><><

LAURA DISAPPEARED before I got up the next morning, and she didn't come back until dinnertime. I tried to tell myself it was okay. I'd do my research, and she'd do whatever it was she was doing.

I looked up some physics articles on the Internet that dealt with the theory of time. I needed to know if it was possible that the past existed at the same time as the present. Maybe it is possible to break through linear time and glimpse the past. Most science makes some sense to me. But these articles were so abstract and complicated—they were mostly pages and pages of formulas—that I could barely follow them. I was actually relieved when my parents came home late that afternoon and spent an hour complaining about airport delays. *That* I could understand.

I had just started to tell them about Laura when she breezed in and sat down for the grilled salmon and potatoes my mom had made for dinner. I was worried about what they would say. I'd never had a girl staying at the house before, but my parents hardly even blinked. She totally charmed them. By the end of dinner my mother had invited her to stay as long as she wanted.

I was glad Laura was going to stick around. I couldn't help hoping that she was the key to some part of the whole Blair puzzle. And I was getting kind of used to seeing her every day.

The next morning Laura tried to slip out again before I was awake. But I was ready for her. I trailed her into town, no problem. She turned down a side street and by the time I got there—no more than fifteen seconds later—she had vanished entirely.

I raced down the street, checking every possible point of escape.

But she was gone. Poof.

Instinct and logic told me Laura was headed for the woods, so I hurried there—and tried in vain to track her. I shouted her name until I was hoarse. I studied the trail for any sign of her. All I found was a strange hole, dug deep in the earth, just off the trail to the Parr house. It definitely hadn't been there a few days before.

I left the woods just before dusk. She came home after dark and slipped into the basement without even saying hello to my parents.

That night I headed down to the basement and knocked on the door.

"Laura, we need to talk," I said when she came to

meet me, dressed in her bathrobe. She was dirty again. As if she'd been smearing earth on her face. What was she doing out there in those woods?

"Not tonight," she said. "I have to take a shower, and I don't feel well. Sorry, Cade—really. I've got to go straight to bed."

A while later my mom complained that all our big carving knives were missing.

"All of them?" I said slowly. I immediately thought of Laura. I couldn't help it.

I ran to my room and dug around in my dresser for the Swiss Army knife I'd had since I was a kid.

It was gone, too.

That did it, I decided. I wasn't going to let Laura put me off any longer. She was in trouble. She needed help. My help.

I went back downstairs. The door to the basement's bathroom was closed, and I could hear the shower running. I decided I was going to just sit there and wait for Laura to come out, when I noticed her backpack right next to the cot. In the outer pocket I could see the outlines of what looked like several large knives.

I'm not proud of what I did next. I know I had no right to go through Laura's pack. I believe everyone's entitled to privacy. But I was also sure those were my mother's carving knives, and I didn't want my mother to suspect Laura or start searching for them on her own.

I unzipped the outer pocket of the pack and gave a low whistle. Laura had taken all four carving knives. Plus my Swiss Army gizmo. I pulled them out.

That was when I saw something else in there. A thin black spiral-bound notebook with the word *Journal* scrawled on the cover in silver ink.

I just held it for a moment. I wanted desperately to read it. To finally know what Laura was seeing and feeling. To find out what was happening when she disappeared into the woods. To know if she was really unlocking the secrets of the Black Hills.

But reading someone's journal had to be the ultimate sleazy act. When I started my investigations, I promised myself I'd never stoop to tactics like that. Every bit of information I got, I had to get legitimately.

Besides, I had to return those knives and figure out a story that my mom would buy.

I put the journal back, went back up to the kitchen, and carefully set the knives in the bottom drawer of the cabinet next to the sink. Then I also moved some pots to the wrong shelf.

My mother walked into the kitchen a few minutes later. "I don't understand it," she said. "I've looked for those knives everywhere. Where on earth could they have gone?"

"Why don't you let me look?" I suggested.

I made an elaborate production of checking every cabinet and drawer in the kitchen. "What are *these* doing here?" I asked when I got to the pots on the wrong shelf. Finally I opened the bottom drawer. "Found 'em," I reported.

My mother narrowed her eyes. "I swear, I looked in that drawer. I must be losing my mind."

"You probably looked in all the other drawers," I told her.

"Well, how did they get in the bottom drawer in the first place? You know they belong in the top one."

"But Laura doesn't," I explained. "I cooked up some steaks the other night, and Laura did the cleanup. I guess she just put things away where she *thought* they went. I should have helped her. Sorry."

My mother gave me a weary smile. "No harm done," she said. She dropped a kiss on my head. "I'm going to sleep. Don't stay up too late."

"I won't," I told her. I was relieved that I'd pulled it off. But I also felt weird about lying to my mom and covering up for Laura. What exactly was I covering up? I wondered. What was Laura doing with all those knives? Some part of my brain knew this was genuinely scary. Dangerous. When a houseguest starts stealing knives, you tell that person to leave before they can use them. But I couldn't tell Laura to leave. She was drowning, and I was determined to save her.

I went back downstairs. Laura was sitting on the cot, toweling off her hair. She wore a T-shirt with the sleeves cut off and faded green sweats. She shot me an annoyed look. "Don't I get any privacy around here?"

"Not when you go borrowing my mom's carving knives without telling anyone. She noticed they were gone."

Laura's face went pale. "What did she say?"

"I put them back. And convinced her that they just got misplaced."

"Thank you."

"You're welcome, I think." I stared into her blue eyes. They looked scared. "Laura, please, tell me what's going on. Why did you take four carving knives and my pocketknife? I'm not mad at you or anything, but I need to know—what were you doing with them?"

Laura sighed and pushed a shock of damp hair out of her face. Her shoulders slumped as if she were a criminal who'd been caught, but she turned to face me.

"Look, Cade, I can't explain it. I'm scared half out of my skin most of the time. I can't really tell you what's going on. I'm not sure myself. But I've got to follow my instincts, okay? You've got to trust me."

It occurred to me that maybe she was cutting herself. I'd seen a TV program about that recently. Some people who are really scared of being hurt by the rest of the world hurt themselves first. That way they feel like they at least have control over the hurting.

I glanced at Laura's arms. They were lovely, soft, and long. There wasn't a cut in sight.

Then I noticed the main compartment of her backpack gaping open. A bunch of black candles were stuffed inside.

Oh, man. Standard witchcraft stuff. What was she doing—spells?

"Look, Laura," I said. "I want to help you. But you've got to come clean with me. Now."

She didn't say anything for a while, and when she finally did speak, her voice sounded small and fragile. Like a little girl's. "I can't make it stop, Cade. I can't stop seeing those movies."

I thought back to stuff she'd told me earlier. "You said you always had dreams about the Black Hills and the Blair Witch. Maybe it's your dreams—"

"No! I know the difference between waking and dreaming. These aren't dreams. They're scenes I see inside my head. And they're real in a way that dreams never are."

"Okay." I sat down on the edge of the cot. "Let's

take this one step at a time. I want to understand what's happening to you."

"You can't," she said bleakly. "Unless you're inside my head, you can't possibly understand what it's like."

I rubbed my eyes and tried to figure out another way—a calm, rational way—to approach this.

"All right, maybe I can't understand. But I want to help you. So tell me whatever you can. Like, do you have any idea why this is happening to you?"

Laura wrapped her arms around herself and shook her head. "I don't know why I'm here. I don't know what she wants."

"She?"

"On Sunday, when you and Mr. Mellon went off, the projector started rewinding on its own. The film wasn't blank anymore. It showed me a movie. And I've seen other scenes since then." Laura squeezed her eyes shut. "I know this sounds crazy, but I think when we lived in Burkittsville, when I was a baby, I was taken by the Blair Witch."

I felt my heart begin to beat faster and reminded myself that maybe this was true, and maybe it was a hallucination or a false memory. After all, I didn't know anything about Laura's home life. My research had shown me that sometimes kids don't want to remember their parents hitting them or hurting them. So they remember the hurt coming from someone else. What if that was the case with Laura? What if the Blair Witch was a stand-in for her mother?

"I was in the woods with my parents," she went on. "And I was being held by someone, a stranger. I heard my mother scream at someone to give me back. And then I remembered that I'd gone to the hospital much later—when I was three. My mother told me it was to have a scar from a tractor accident removed."

She opened her eyes and stared at me. "But I know that was a lie, Cade. There was no tractor accident. That day in the woods the witch caught me, and she put her mark on my forehead. That was what was surgically removed."

I swallowed hard. "So you think that's your connection—"

She nodded. "It's why I've always dreamed about this place. That's why I had to come back. But now that I'm here, I don't understand what I'm supposed to do. Except I can't stop seeing all this stuff—"

She put her hands to her eyes, and her whole body began to shake. "When she put her mark on me, she cursed me. Cade, I'm so scared. I'm caught in the curse of the Blair Witch."

I rubbed her back, kind of awkwardly. "It's okay," I told her. "You're not alone in this. I'm going to help you. We'll put all the pieces together and figure out what's going on. We'll find a way to break the curse. It's going to get better."

"You really think so?" she sobbed.

"Definitely," I told her, and wondered when I'd turned into such an accomplished liar.

15

My alarm went off at five-thirty the next morning. I'm not usually an early riser, but I wanted to make certain I was up before Laura. If she set off for the woods again, I was going to follow her. After her confession the night before, I knew it was dangerous to let her go off on her own.

But when I checked downstairs, her bed was empty.

I stood staring at the cot, feeling sick. Laura was out there by herself. Seeing visions that terrified her. Convinced that she was caught in the spell of the Blair Witch. Which, I had to admit, was a real possibility. And even if she wasn't under some kind of curse, I knew how dangerous those woods could be.

I debated for a minute about taking off after her.

But the last time I'd done that, it had been completely useless. Maybe there was something else I could do that would get me closer to the truth.

I decided to call her parents. Not to rat on her or anything. I needed to know what the story was with that scar. Was it really some kind of curse?

I gave Laura's parents till eight A.M. I didn't want to ambush them too early. The phone rang four times before anyone picked it up.

"Hello, Mrs. Morely?" I said.

"Who's calling, please?" The woman was curt. Screening out telephone salespeople, I figured.

"This is Cade Merrill. I'm a friend of Laura's," I answered. "We met through a Web site on the Internet." That didn't sound too good, I guess. But I figured it was best to be as up front as possible.

"Oh—hello, Cade." The voice was nicer now, but still not very friendly. "I believe I've read a magazine article about you. You're the young man in Maryland with those Blair Witch files, right?"

"Right."

There was a long pause. "Well, Laura isn't here," Mrs. Morely said finally. "I know she talked about spending some time in Burkittsville this summer, but she decided to go somewhere else instead."

She decided? I wondered. I remember Laura telling me that her parents had made a stink about her visiting the Black Hills.

"Right," I said quickly. "But actually I was calling to talk to you. Mrs. Morely, can I ask you a few questions?"

Another silence.

"I was just wondering," I went on quickly. "Laura told me once, in an e-mail, about a scar on her forehead, from a tractor accident. I'm doing some research, and I wondered if you could remember the shape of the scar."

Silence again.

Deathly silence.

I could feel the hostility oozing through the phone.

But I waited. It's a trick I've learned—let the other person be the one to speak first.

"I don't know what you're talking about," Laura's mother finally said in an icy tone.

My mind started to race, considering the possibilities. There were basically two. Either Laura had made the whole story up—or her mother was hiding something.

"Laura, uh, never had a scar on her forehead?" I repeated. "Because she definitely told me she was in some kind of tractor accident, and went to the hospital later to have the scar removed. But hey, if you can't remember the shape of the scar, maybe the surgeon can," I added pointedly. I knew I was playing hardball here, but there was no other way.

"None of that ever happened," Mrs. Morely said firmly. "I can't imagine why Laura would tell you that."

She was clearly uncomfortable, which made me think that she—not Laura—was the one who was lying. I could hear it in her voice. In fact, she sounded like she might be about to cut the conversation off.

"Mrs. Morely," I said, trying to keep her on the phone. "One more question. Can you tell me what year your family moved from Maryland to Minnesota?"

More silence.

"You know, I'm sorry, Cade, but I don't feel comfortable answering these questions, and I have no idea why this pertains to any kind of research. I don't even know you. Maybe you can talk to Laura sometime when she comes back home."

I knew I was about to lose her, but I still had one question to ask Laura's mom. An important one.

"Does Laura have a history of any kind of mental illness?" I blurted out.

The silence on the other end of the line was so cold, you could almost feel the jet stream dipping down from the Arctic Circle.

"No, of course not," Mrs. Morely said huffily. "Why on earth would you ask me something like that?"

I thought fast. "Well, I've gotten some, uh, strange

e-mails from her lately," I answered. "And I was . . . I was just worried about her."

That seemed to get her attention. "Strange how?"

"She just sounds . . . distant. Like she's pulling away from people or something," I said, telling as much of the truth as I could.

"Thank you for your concern. I have nothing further to add," Mrs. Morely said. Then she hung up.

I clicked off the phone and tossed it onto my bed.

My mind was reeling, trying to sort things out.

It boiled down to one point that could clear up a lot of the others: Had Laura even *had* a scar removed? That should be simple enough to find out.

I sent an e-mail to a friend of mine at the FBI (I call him Ted the Fed since I cannot reveal his real name) and told him I needed to see any medical records he could dig up on Laura Morely, especially any hospitalizations or surgeries in the early eighties.

And I needed it fast.

Then I made another decision. One I didn't feel so good about. I always said I'd be aboveboard and honest in my research. I always said I'd respect the privacy of anyone involved in my investigations. Now I was about to cross a line and violate all those fine ideals.

But I was desperate. Laura had given me a story that I wanted to believe but couldn't risk accepting without some hard proof. Her mother had given me nothing.

If I was going to help Laura, I had to know what was really going on. So I went back down to the basement.

And I opened her journal.

16

Two things about Laura's journal hit me right away.

One: It had a strange smell. I couldn't identify it, but the odor was putrid, like some kind of chemical.

Two: Some of the pages were stuck together. When I pried them apart, it seemed as if they had been stuck together with blood.

No words were written on those two pages—just symbols. They had been drawn in some thick dark liquid, probably blood that had oxidized to brown.

I recognized the symbols right away—like the hieroglyphics on the walls of Rustin Parr's house, they were part of the ancient language of witchcraft called Transitus Fluvii. There were other symbols, too—crude drawings of the ancient Futhark language. Both of these languages were associated with the Blair Witch legend. I was tempted to translate them then and there, using the decoder I'd formulated in my database, but then the journal fell open to a page near the end.

Just a few minutes ago, when I was standing in the shower, I saw that night again. It's weird how every time I see it, there's one thing I can never see— the witch herself. Not even her face or her hands. But this time I heard her voice. "Only eighteen months old and you put up such a struggle!" She was laughing at me. "You're a strong one, Laura Morely, a fighter. And so I take you for my own." Then I saw myself pushed down onto my back, held against the forest floor. And I saw the point of a blade slice through the skin of my forehead.

After that, the handwriting on the page got so shaky, I couldn't read it all.
I flipped to another page.

I can't shut out the voices. They're with me all the time. They say there's only one way to save myself. Go to the woods. Light the candles. Say the words. Do their bidding. Tonight I cut my feet and drank my

*own blood. Am I insane? I see those twins all the
time. Even here, at Cade's house. The images won't
stop. . . .*

*One thing I know for sure. It started when I went
to that house. As soon as I stepped across the foundation, it was like I'd crossed a line. Rustin Parr is
everywhere. I can hear him laughing and his brother
screaming. I can't keep living this way. I feel like I'm
going mad.*

I read the whole journal, or at least the parts that
were legible. Page after page filled with Laura's fears.
That she was going crazy. That she couldn't stop the
visions or the voices. And that she couldn't stop herself from going to the woods.

When I finally stopped reading, I was more confused than ever. A while ago I did some Internet
research on schizophrenia. I read a bunch of first-
person accounts from people who suffered from the
disease. Almost all of them heard voices. Maybe
Laura Morely *was* going insane.

But I had seen those photographs of the Parr
house with my own eyes, I reminded myself. And
from the start something about Laura had convinced
me that she was telling the truth. I didn't believe
that it was an act or an illness. My gut told me she
was right. She was an innocent, caught in the evil
that runs through Black Hills Forest.

I took the journal up to my room and started translating the symbols. It took a while, because Laura's representation of them was crude and parts seemed to be missing.

But I'm pretty sure they translated as:

To see too much . . . to die too soon.

I stared at the journal page. No wonder Laura was terrified. Withdrawn. Silent.

But maybe Laura didn't know what the symbols meant. She could have copied them from somewhere, and . . .

The phone rang.

"Hello?" I said, a little impatiently.

"Cade? It's Danny. What's up, man? Want to play some one-on-one?"

Danny is a good friend of mine. I've been pretty busy lately with my research, so I haven't seen too much of him since school let out. I was going to say no, but my head was swimming with trying to figure out the whole Laura situation. Maybe a little fun would do me good.

"Sure," I said. "I'll meet you at school." We usually shot baskets on the asphalt court outside the elementary school.

"Okay, see you in fifteen," Danny said.

I pulled on a pair of shorts, changed T-shirts,

and hopped into the Morris Minor. A few minutes later I pulled into the parking lot at the elementary school.

A bunch of parents and their kids were crawling all over the climbing structures. Two boys were playing catch. A little girl in a pink dress was stuck at the top of the slide, crying and refusing to go down.

"Cade! Over here, man!" Danny called. He stood bouncing the ball on the blacktop beyond the wood-chip-covered playground.

I started toward him. That was when I saw some-one—a teenage girl—get up from a kneeling position near two kids and dart away. As if she was trying to hide.

My gaze followed the fleeing girl. The stiff clumps of blond hair were unmistakable.

"Laura?" I called.

She disappeared behind the line of bushes that edged the playground. I checked through the branches. No one was there.

I turned and gazed around the playground. The two kids she'd been talking to were Max and Evan, the Willoughby twins. They looked a little bewil-dered at having been deserted like that, and they hadn't seen me.

"Yo, Cade!"

Danny was getting impatient.

"Just a sec! Be right there!" I called.

I scanned the crowd of parents and spotted Angela Willoughby sitting on a bench. I jogged over to her.

"Uh, hi," I said, interrupting her conversation with another mother. "Sorry to butt in, but I was just wondering—do you know that girl, Laura Morely, who's been staying with us for a while?"

Mrs. Willoughby nodded. "I've seen her once or twice."

"Have you seen her today?" I asked. "I mean, here?"

She shrugged. "I'm not sure. She might have walked through a while ago. Why?"

"I thought I saw her talking to your boys," I answered.

"Could have been," the twins' mom said, shrugging again. "She was here yesterday, playing with Max and Evan. She seemed very sweet."

For some reason it made me nervous to think about Laura with those two little boys. Especially since she'd told me she didn't like kids.

My mind started making horrible leaps. What if the normal Laura had no interest in kids, but now that the voices were telling her what to do . . .

Should I warn Mrs. Willoughby about Laura?

"Cade!" Danny was getting annoyed.

I gave the bushes one more look. I wanted to catch up with Laura—wherever she had gone. But

127

the twins were fine. And I'd see Laura at home. No point in raising an alarm with no proof.

I shot baskets with Danny for the next forty minutes. He beat me 24–8. My heart wasn't in it, I guess.

When I got home, I was surprised to find Laura in the kitchen. My parents were out, and she had made spaghetti and meatballs for the two of us. The whole house smelled great. And Laura was glowing.

I felt almost guilty over some of the thoughts I'd had about her. But then I remembered her journal. I thought about Laura writing that she had drunk her own blood.

"Dinner's almost ready," she said. "Have you got any wine?"

"Uh, not open, I guess. My family doesn't really drink."

"Okay." She shrugged and shot me a grin that said "Too bad."

I was a little stunned as we sat down at the table and Laura served the salad, acting all happy and homemaker-ish. I swear she was even humming.

"Well, you're in a good mood," I said, reaching for the Parmesan cheese. "So where have you been all day, anyway?"

"Oh, I just took a nice long walk," she answered. "This whole curse thing has been blowing my mind, so I thought I'd better clear my head."

I took a bite of salad. It was great—she'd put in

avocados and toasted almonds and bits of bacon. "Where'd you go?" I asked.

"I don't know, just walked." She sounded slightly tense. "Down past the river and back. Why?"

"I saw you at the playground," I said.

Laura's head snapped up. "What playground?" she said, frowning.

"Near the Morgan School," I answered.

She shook her head and went back to eating. "Nope. I wasn't there."

"Are you sure?" I said.

She dropped her fork loudly on her plate. "Am I *sure* about where I was? Yeah, I'm sure. What's *that* supposed to mean?"

"Look, Laura, I'm really worried about you," I said. "You're getting sucked into this whole thing—and I don't know where it's going to end."

"I'm not!" she insisted. "Can't you see I'm trying to get over it? Why can't we just drop the subject for one night?"

That was fair enough. I could tell that Laura was trying to shake off the dark feelings that had made her so withdrawn for the past few days. It was hard to imagine why else she'd be sitting there across the table from me in my mom's chef apron.

It seemed like I should tell her that I had called her mom, though. And that her mom had denied the whole tractor story.

Later, I decided. After dinner. Why spoil the big meal that Laura had spent so much time fussing over?

It could wait.

That was what I thought, anyway.

I had no idea that my window of opportunity was about to close.

Time was running out for Laura Morely.

17

That night was one of those soft, balmy, crystal-clear evenings when all the stars sparkle and the world seems hushed. There was a full moon, too. Maybe that was why Laura and I both got a little carried away.

Laura and I had had a pretty great time—as if we were really close friends. No, more than friends. It was almost like a date. Delicious dinner. Amazing conversation. Even some definite romance in the air.

We watched a video, some foreign film she'd rented. It was funny, sexy, and light—just what we needed.

And then I started to kiss her. It was unbelievable. Laura felt it, too. I could tell. But she suddenly pulled away and put the lights back on. The spell was instantly broken. For some reason, I didn't feel that disappointed. Laura Morely probably wasn't the sort of person I should get too involved with.

Needless to say, I didn't mention my phone conversation with her mother. We just said good night and that was it.

At one A.M., I heard our back door opening and someone creeping down the driveway.

No way, I thought. You're not getting away from me this time.

I hustled to pull on some jeans and a T-shirt, stumbling over the pile of dirty clothes on my bedroom floor. Then I jammed my feet into my running shoes and hauled myself out of there.

I followed her as quietly as I could. It was easy to stay out of sight. I knew all the places to duck in so she wouldn't spot me.

When she turned left on Route 17, toward the woods, my heart skipped a beat. She was going into Black Hills Forest in the middle of the night. *No one* did that—not on purpose, anyway. It was almost impossible to find your way in the dark, because the landmarks weren't that visible.

I couldn't figure out whether Laura was the bravest or the craziest person I'd ever met.

She turned off the road and onto the trail, flipping

on a small flashlight. A thin beam of light stretched to the ground.

Great. *She* could see where we were going.

My pulse raced, pumped. This must be how Heather felt, I thought. In the woods, in the dark. Half-hoping, half-fearing that the evil would present itself.

I followed the sound of Laura's footsteps. With the moon I could see the trail at my feet—sort of. But that was all.

After a while Laura began to run.

This is nuts, I thought. But I ran, too. I had to, if I wanted to keep up with her.

Finally she stopped.

I crouched on the trail, panting. We'd both been moving pretty fast.

That was when I heard a voice, in the distance.

Chanting.

The words weren't clear, and it was definitely some other language. Nothing I'd ever heard before.

I listened harder.

It was Laura's voice.

"Laura?" I called.

Immediately the chanting stopped.

"Laura, it's me, Cade. Where are you? What are you doing?"

No answer.

I knew if I could hear her, she could hear me.

"Laura, come on, answer me."

I took a few steps forward.

"I talked to your mom today."

I thought for sure that would get her.

But she still didn't answer.

"Laura?" Silence. "I'm giving you five minutes to come back here. Please. This is dangerous. Come on—five minutes. Then I'm going for the police."

That was a lie. I stayed there in the woods, crouched on the trail, for the next hour and a half. I was waiting to see if she'd start chanting again, or what.

But the silence continued. She must have known I was still there.

Finally I gave up and started home.

But as I made my way down the path, a shaft of moonlight fell through a space in the trees, lighting up something on the ground.

I stopped and bent to see what it was.

My stomach churned.

It was an animal—a raccoon—that had been completely disemboweled. The creature's heart and liver were lying a foot away, placed near a pile of carefully arranged stones.

Like the piles of stones in Heather's footage.

Then I heard the chanting again. Traveling through the night, in the dark.

I'm almost positive it was her.

I listened hard, and I realized there were two voices chanting. Laura's voice and one that sounded hoarse and much older.

My body went stiff with terror. For a moment all I could think was that the Blair Witch had her.

You don't know that, I told myself. I made myself take several deep breaths and let them out slowly. You don't know anything until you see it with your own eyes.

I wanted desperately to run, to get out of the forest. But I couldn't leave Laura that way. I forced myself to move closer to the source of the chanting, completely aware that if I found it, I might never make it out of the forest again.

I stumbled through the woods. The sound seemed closer one minute, farther the next.

"Laura!" I shouted again. "Where are you?"

The two voices rose in a thin, eerie harmony.

I turned toward the left. I didn't even know where the path was anymore, and I didn't care. All I cared about was finding them. While Laura was still alive.

At last I was sure that I really was closer to them. The sound was definitely louder. In a clearing filled with moonlight I saw something hanging from a low branch of a maple tree. A stickman. It bobbed up and down in rhythm with the chanting.

Suddenly the chanting stopped. The silence was

worse. I have never experienced such silence. I walked forward. Each step I took sounded like a crash of cymbals. I kept walking, deeper into the woods. Deeper into the mystery. I had to keep walking. I wasn't sure why, but I was desperate to keep going—desperate to see something—but what?

A cloud crossed in front of the moon. I was in total darkness now. *Only a crazy person would go into the woods at night.* My own words echoed in my head. I realized I'd never find Laura or anything else in the pitch dark. I made my way back and took the stickman off the tree. It gave off the same rotten odor as Laura's journal.

Then the adrenaline kicked in and I ran like hell.

PART V:

The Twins

Based on the notes and recollections of Cade Merrill
and conversations with Laura Morely

18

After I got home that night, I turned on every light in the living room and sat on the couch, waiting for Laura. I couldn't get that terrifying scene in the woods out of my head. The disemboweled raccoon. The stickman bobbing up and down. Had Laura put it there so I would find it? Was it supposed to throw me off her track or help me find her? And what had happened to Laura? I prayed she would soon be home safe. At four-thirty A.M., I finally crashed.

The next morning was Friday. I threw on a T-shirt and jeans and came downstairs to find my father at the table.

He glanced up from his newspaper. "I'm glad

you're up," he said. "I want to talk to you about your guest."

I didn't even know if "my guest" had survived the night.

Don't grill me now, Dad, I thought. I can't answer any of your questions.

"I heard her come in a couple of hours ago," he said. "Your mom and I are concerned."

I tried to look as unconcerned as possible. Inside I was nearly collapsing with relief. "Laura . . . just has trouble sleeping," I improvised. I was doing it again. Lying to my folks. Then again, what choice did I have? She was in trouble and I had to help her. "When Laura can't sleep, she gets up and takes a walk. She says it's sort of a game that helps her relax. It's no big deal, Dad."

My father raised one eyebrow. "Laura is our guest, Cade. If something happened to her, we'd be responsible."

Maybe you're not, I was thinking. Maybe this has nothing to do with you at all.

"Where does Laura live?" my father went on.

"Minnesota. She explained that to you the night you came home from vacation."

"Well, perhaps it's time she returned to Minnesota."

I nearly choked on my OJ. Laura was in no shape to be put on a plane. "Dad, you don't understand—"

"On the contrary." My father interrupted me. "Your mother and I have been very understanding. We've allowed you to spend countless hours on your research. We've allowed you to take in this young woman whom we know next to nothing about. But this house isn't a hotel, and whatever it is Laura's up to isn't a game."

"You don't think I know all that?"

"There's something about Laura that isn't right." My father was speaking quietly, but he was dead serious. "I think she might be dangerous, Cade. I want you to tell her she has to leave."

A part of me knew he was right, but I couldn't hear it. I was in too deep. I shot out of my seat. "You don't know the first thing about her! She's my friend, and she needs my help, and she's not going anywhere!"

"Cade!"

"Shhh!" I glanced toward the basement door, which was standing open. "She'll hear you," I whispered.

"Huh?" My dad followed my gaze. "Oh—no, she won't. She went out again about twenty minutes ago. I think I saw her heading across the street, toward the Willoughbys'."

"What?"

I raced out of the kitchen and dashed to the front window.

Sure enough, Laura was kneeling on the Willoughbys' front lawn. Her head was bent low to Max and Evan, just the way I'd seen her on the playground yesterday, as if she was telling them a secret or something. Then she offered something small to Evan, and he threw his arms around her neck in a big hug.

A chill ran up my back, seeing Laura with those boys again. What was she doing?

I couldn't help feeling weird about her hanging around little kids like that, especially knowing she'd been chanting and who knows what else in the woods last night. It just wasn't right.

I pushed out through the front door and raced forward.

But a minivan was coming down the street, and I couldn't cross.

"Laura!" I called.

Her head snapped up, and a scowl spread over her face. Then she scrambled to her feet and grabbed the two boys by the hands, hurrying them around the side of the house.

"Laura, don't do that!" I shouted, dodging another car.

Finally I made it across the road and ran around to the back of the Willoughbys' house.

The yard was empty, so I sprinted around to the front again.

"Max! Evan!" I called.

No answer. The front yard was empty, too.

Figuring they'd gone in the house, I rang the doorbell.

That was when I noticed that the driveway was empty. Both of the Willoughbys' cars were gone.

That doesn't make sense, I thought. If the parents are gone, the boys wouldn't be left home alone . . . unless the Willoughbys asked Laura to baby-sit?

I should have warned Mrs. Willoughby in the playground, I thought.

I rang the bell again, then pounded on the door.

There was no response.

I circled the house once more, looking for an open window. If they're inside, they're hiding, I decided. But there were no signs of life anywhere.

Slowly I crossed the road again, back to our side of the street. Then I turned and stared at the Willoughby house from our front yard.

"Okay, Laura," I said. "Where are you?" And whose voice are you listening to? I added silently.

I suddenly realized how completely panicked I was. My heart was racing, my chest muscles were constricted, my stomach was in knots. Panic is not a trustworthy state. When you're panicked, terror rules your brain. Which means not many people think clearly then.

So maybe it *wasn't* Laura, I allowed. I took more

deep breaths, forcing the panic away. Maybe the Willoughbys had a blond-haired baby-sitter, and that was the person I'd seen with the boys. The least I could do was check our basement and make sure that Laura wasn't there.

I pelted back into the house and down to the basement. "Laura?" I called.

There was no answer.

I glanced around the basement. Laura wasn't there. But her journal lay on the cot open to her latest entry.

This time I didn't even hesitate. I just started reading.

> *I know I'm in hell. Everywhere I look, I see evil. The voices are with me always. Except tonight. We had dinner—I even let him kiss me. He's a cool guy, but he doesn't get it. He never will because he can't see the truth. How can he be so clueless about the fact that he's living across the street from the next incarnation of horror? A twin who will perpetuate the evil. The curse. Unless I stop him. Is that why she brought me here?*
>
> *To stop the strong one by killing him? By offering him to her?*
>
> *Is there any other way?*
>
> *Will that act save me?*

It's my only hope. She says if I keep going to the woods, I'll find an answer.

Even as I write this, I'm seeing the images, hearing the words. She wants me to go there again today—with them. If I don't go, I will die.

I'm so tired. I just want to sleep.

But I can't.

I can't.

I can't.

✄✄✄

I FLEW OUT OF THE HOUSE again and made a beeline for the Willoughbys'. Once again, I started pounding on their door.

I nearly fell over with astonishment when the door opened. Angela Willoughby stood there, blinking sleepily.

"Cade," she said. She rubbed at her eyes. "I was just lying down for a few minutes. I woke up with a killer headache this morning."

"Where are Max and Evan?" I blurted out.

She blinked again. "They're sitting in front of the TV, eating peanut butter and jelly sandwiches."

"Are you sure?"

"Cade, what is this?" she asked.

My heart was still hammering, and I sort of felt like I was making a fool of myself. Except that I couldn't ignore what I'd just seen in Laura's journal.

"Um, it's Laura, my friend who's staying at my house. She's not feeling well. My mom thinks she might have the mumps or something contagious. So she asked me to tell you that you should make sure Laura doesn't get too close to the kids."

Great, Cade. Blame your mother.

"Okay," Angela said. "Thanks for letting me know."

She closed the door.

I was still shaking. I'd been so sure I was going to find horrible trouble.

19

Laura looked as if she hadn't slept or eaten for days when she knocked on my bedroom door late that night.

I was at the computer, sending another e-mail to Ted the Fed. Why hadn't he come up with those medical records on Laura Morely yet? I wanted to know.

Her knock startled me. I clicked on my screen-saver so she wouldn't see that I was writing about her.

"Yeah?" I said.

She came in, kind of hesitantly. Like I said, she looked awful.

I tried to remember how pretty and excited she'd

been that first day, when I picked her up at the motel. Like she was at the start of a fabulous adventure.

"Can I sit down?"

I already knew that Max and Evan Willoughby were safe. I'd talked to their mother again just a couple of hours ago.

I turned to face Laura.

"What's up?" I asked cautiously.

Laura sat down on my bed and stared at the floor for a moment. Then she looked me square in the eyes.

"I need to borrow your car," she said.

"What for?" I asked.

"I can't tell you," she answered.

I sighed. "Well, then, I can't let you borrow it, Laura. You've been pretty weird lately. Something's wrong—you know that, don't you? You're in over your head. Even my parents are worried about you." I hesitated before saying, "I think you need help. Maybe the professional kind."

Laura hung her head. "I know," she said softly. "But this is all going to end soon. You've got to trust me. Please."

"How can I trust you if you won't tell me what you've been up to?" I shot back.

She shook her head.

148

I leaned forward. "Please, Laura. Tell me what you've been doing. I need to know, and maybe I can help. Besides—how can it *hurt* to tell me?"

She thought about that for a moment. I could see her considering the idea and struggling with herself. Finally her face broke, as if she'd finally let go.

"I see visions," she whispered. "All the time."

"What kind of visions?" I asked carefully, trying not to scare her off.

"All kinds. At first it was just when I went into the woods. Seeing Rustin and Dale Parr as kids, always fighting. Rustin killed his twin brother. You know that already, right? From your research and everything?" Her eyes were pleading.

I cleared my throat. "Uh, no, Laura. I didn't."

"Rustin killed Dale. I saw it—or part of it, anyway. It wasn't a hunting accident. He bashed his brother's head in with a rock." Her voice trembled and rose as she told me the whole story. "You believe me, don't you?" she finished. She sounded hysterical by now.

"Yes," I said.

And I did, in a way. I knew that something had hold of Laura. Was using her for its purposes. How could I trust what the voices were telling her?

"I know you're not lying to me," I said carefully. "But I don't know if we should trust the visions.

Maybe what you saw was . . . some sort of hallucination. Just because you see these visions doesn't make them true."

"I saw myself as a baby, with that scar!" she cried. "I *know* it was true! I can feel it! The witch took me and put a curse on me, in the woods."

"But your mom said . . . ," I began, then quickly stopped. I'd forgotten I hadn't told Laura about my conversation with her mother yet.

Laura stared at me. "Why would you believe *her*? She's been lying to me all along. And now . . ." Her voice trailed off.

"Tell me," I urged.

I thought I already knew what she was going to say. I'd read her journal. But I wanted to hear it from Laura's own lips.

"I saw . . ." She stopped.

"What?" I held my breath.

Her face twisted, as if she was too horrified to say the words. "The Willoughby twins," she whispered. "I saw Max setting fire to a house—to Rustin Parr's house in the woods. And Evan was inside!"

She was on the verge of crying.

"But that can't be right." I tried to sound reasonable, rational. "That house burned down years ago, remember? The only one who sees it for real—or unreal—is you. Besides—I know those kids. Max is a little rambunctious, that's all. He'd never do anything really dangerous like that, believe me."

"But I saw it," Laura insisted. "I *saw* Max set the fire. He was trying to *kill* his brother! It's just like Rustin and Dale all over again!"

"What do you mean?" I asked, frowning.

"Isn't it obvious?" she said, throwing up her hands. "Don't you get it, Cade?"

"Not really. Tell me."

"It's the twin thing—history repeating itself. One of those boys is *evil*," she whispered, leaning into my face. "Don't you see that? And the other one is good. She wants the evil one to survive, to be hers."

I drew away in horror. What Laura was saying sounded totally crazy.

But her voice was filled with conviction, a power that was hard to deny.

She sounded so certain that she was telling the truth.

No, I told myself. I know Max and Evan. They're good kids. There's nothing evil about either one of them.

No weird eyes. No sinister smiles.

And no scar.

"So can I borrow your car?" Laura asked.

I looked at her for a long moment. "What for? You've got to tell me where you're going."

"I can't." She shook her head decisively.

I shrugged. "Then I can't let you take it, Laura. Sorry. I'm too worried about you. And I want you to stay away from those twins, okay?"

"Fine." Laura stood up and marched to the door. "It doesn't matter. I'll go tomorrow. It won't happen tonight, anyway."

Then she walked out.

20

The next morning, Saturday, Laura woke me early. Politely.

"Cade?"

I quickly pulled on some clothes and opened the door. "Yeah? What's up?"

She looked different. Almost happy. She seemed almost normal.

"I'm going home," she said brightly. "Now can I borrow your car?"

"To drive home?" I stared at her in surprise.

"No, silly." She laughed and gave me a playful punch on the shoulder. "I just want to go to the bus station to buy a ticket. Then I'll come back and get my things."

I hesitated. Was Laura just playing with me? She had to be. I couldn't believe she'd changed so quickly. Back to the determined, high-energy, driven girl I'd met just a week ago.

"Uh, I'm not sure," I said. "Besides, you don't need to buy bus tickets in advance. It's not like they're going to sell out."

Her face darkened. "Look, Cade, I just need the car. For an hour." Her voice was forceful again—demanding, almost threatening. "And then I'll be out of your life, and you won't have to think about me ever again."

What were the chances of *that*? I wondered.

"See?" Laura added, pointing to her backpack and camera bags out in the hall. "I'm already packed."

"I'll take you," I offered.

"Fine." Her voice was cold. "Then I can make an earlier bus."

I thought quickly. I'd promised my dad I'd do some errands for him. And after yesterday's blowup, I figured I should probably just do them and not give him reasons to pick another fight.

"Okay," I told Laura. "I need to do some stuff this morning. "I can take you around eleven."

She didn't look happy with my answer, but she said, "Fine. I'll go make some coffee."

Had I just pissed her off? Probably. Still, that was

better than giving her my car, I decided as I stepped into the shower.

She was really going back to Minnesota. And my feelings about that were complicated. I couldn't help feeling sad. I was going to miss Laura Morely. But I was also relieved that she'd be out of danger. And truthfully, I was a little disappointed. For a while there, I'd been sure we were on the verge of a breakthrough in the Blair Witch legend.

Had any of Laura's "visions" been real?

Yes. I'd seen those photographs in the darkroom with my own eyes—of the Parr family and their house.

All of a sudden I remembered the negatives.

Where were they? I wondered. We had never gone back to print them again.

Was Laura going to take them home with her?

I got out of the shower, dressed, and went down to the kitchen. The coffee machine was doing its drip thing, but Laura was nowhere in sight.

I stared at the camera bags she'd left near the kitchen door, wondering which one had the negatives. Should I search for them? Try to keep them? I'd already compromised all my ethics anyway.

But I didn't get a chance to decide, because just then the doorbell rang.

Someone must have been pretty impatient,

because they kept pushing the bell. I hurried to the front door and opened it.

Angela Willoughby was standing there, looking frantic.

"Have you seen Max or Evan?" she asked.

"No, why?"

"Because I can't find them anywhere!" she cried. "They're gone!"

21

I bolted outside and glanced at our driveway. My heart plummeted to my stomach. The Morris Minor was gone.

I took another look in the kitchen. The hook where I usually hung my keys was empty.

I turned back to Angela Willoughby. "Are you sure they're gone?" I asked her. "Where did you see them last?"

Mrs. Willoughby seemed crazed with worry and fear. "In the backyard," she said. "It's fenced in. They were out there playing in the sandbox, and then all of a sudden they disappeared."

The twins were gone. And Laura had my car.

Mrs. Willoughby ran down the front steps, shouting the boys' names.

"Max! Evan! Max! Where are you?"

"Wait!" I called, following after her. "Did you . . . by any chance . . . see Laura Morely?"

She stopped and shook her head. "No. Max! Evan! Answer Mommy!"

"How long have they been gone?" I asked.

"I don't know. Ten minutes maybe. They can't have gotten far."

"Did you, um, hear anything?" I asked. "I mean . . ." I was reluctant to even say it. "Like a car?"

Mrs. Willoughby's face turned white. "I'm not sure," she said. "Actually, I did hear an engine."

"Do you know if it sounded anything like my car?"

"I didn't notice. Why?"

I knew I had to be honest with her. "Because I have a bad feeling that Laura may have borrowed my car about ten minutes ago."

Her eyes met mine, and she read my thoughts. "Oh, my god," she said. "Do you think she . . . she . . . took them?"

I'm pretty sure the answer was on my face. Yeah. I thought so.

Mrs. Willoughby turned and started running toward the street.

"Max! Answer me!" she screamed frantically.

"Wait!" I called, running to catch up with her. She kept darting from one side of the road to the other, wildly checking in various people's yards.

I grabbed her arm. "I'll help you search," I offered. "Let's split up. I'll take Dover Street, Marlboro, and Edgewood. You take Andover and Elkmont. Meet me in front of your house in ten minutes if you don't find them, because . . . I have another idea."

She nodded, still panicky, and started calling the boys' names again.

"Max!" I shouted, heading in the opposite direction. "Evan!"

But my gut told me we wouldn't find them.

I knew that Laura had taken the boys to the woods.

"Max! Evan! Come on out, guys!" I tried to believe in what we were doing, searching the neighborhood.

Ten minutes later Mrs. Willoughby met up with me in front of her house, looking totally wild-eyed.

"Nothing?" I asked. "Has anyone seen them?"

She shook her head, breathing hard from running the whole time.

"Okay, let's take your car," I said.

"Where?" she asked.

"To Black Hills Forest," I answered, trying not to alarm her.

"Oh, my god." She collapsed against the garage door, obviously imagining the worst.

Mrs. Willoughby had lived here all her life. Everyone for miles around knew about the Blair Witch stories—and about the crazy things that were rumored to happen out in those woods. When children went missing in our area, people always thought the same thing.

"Are you okay to drive?" I asked, taking her arm.

She shook her head and handed me her car keys from her pocket. "You drive." We zoomed toward the woods, probably breaking all the town speed limits. But I knew we needed to get there fast. My fears seemed to be confirmed as we rounded the curve to my usual parking spot—the place where I had parked on that first day with Laura.

The Morris Minor was sitting there, just off the road.

But Laura wasn't in it.

"Oh, no," Angela Willoughby moaned, seeing my empty car and guessing what it meant.

"Don't worry, we'll find them," I said.

We jumped out of the car and ran up the path, calling the boys' names.

"Max! Evan! Boys!"

No answer.

I took the lead, racing past all the landmarks that would lead me to the Parr house site. After about twenty minutes of running, Mrs. Willoughby stopped in the middle of the trail.

"Cade, where are we going?" she demanded.

What was I supposed to tell her? My suspicions were just too weird. You see, Mrs. Willoughby, my friend Laura had this vision about your kids. She saw—or thought she saw—Max setting fire to Rustin Parr's house, which no longer exists, so he could kill his twin brother.

I cleared my throat. "I just have this feeling," I said, "from some things Laura told me. I think we should hike to Rustin Parr's house."

"Is that far?"

"Yes. A couple of hours," I answered. "Look, you call the police. There's a phone booth near where we left the car. And call the rangers' station, too. Wait here for them. But I'm going to the site. I think it's our best chance of finding your boys."

Something in my voice must have scared her. I saw her whirl around, torn between following her own instincts and mine. Finally she headed toward her car.

"I'll be right back," she called.

I started walking faster. I knew I didn't have much time. My heart was pounding and my head was spinning.

What was Laura's plan? I wondered. Was she going to kill Max, to keep him from setting the fire and from hurting his twin? Wasn't that what she'd said in her journal?

Or was it the other way around? Was Laura somehow doing the witch's bidding, just as Rustin Parr had done before her? What was Laura's strange connection to Parr?

I checked my watch. About forty minutes had elapsed since Mrs. Willoughby had rung my bell, plus the ten minutes the boys had been missing before she came over.

They'd been gone almost an hour, I realized.

"Maaax! Evaaan!" I called.

I kept it up, shouting their names every minute or so. But there was no response, no sign of the twins anywhere.

Except for the candy wrapper I found on the trail. It was a Gummi Bear package.

"Evan's favorite," I muttered, picking it up carefully.

"Evan!" I called. "It's me, Cade! Where are you? Answer me!"

But what if he can't? I thought suddenly, remembering Laura's vision.

What if Max was the only one alive?

"Hellllp!"

The sound was small, distant. But it was unmistakably a child's voice.

I froze. "Evan?" I called again.

"Helllp!"

The voice had come from ahead and to my left. I was reluctant to leave the trail, but I had no choice.

I ran toward the sound, pushing aside branches and stumbling over rocks.

"Help me!"

The cry seemed to be coming from the right now—back toward the path. I switched directions. This was crazy.

"Where are you, Evan? Call out again!"

"Here!"

Where?

It was so hard to tell. The sounds *seemed* closer, but the woods were strange. I couldn't say for sure which direction the voice had come from.

I took a guess and ran back through the woods, off the trail, and up over another rise.

My heart stopped. I smelled smoke.

Then I saw it. Black, billowing smoke was coming over the hill like a thick fog. My eyes began to sting and tear. My throat felt dry and constricted, and I began to cough. But I pushed on up the hill. It was very difficult to see anything through the smoke, but I swear it was there. At the top of the hill was Rustin Parr's house. Not just the remains. Not just the old foundation.

The whole house, just as Laura and I had seen it in the darkroom images.

Except that it was burning. Blazing. Flaming out of control.

I stood for a moment, stunned. Laura was right. Her vision had come true!

The black smoke engulfed me, but I raced toward the building. I wiped my eyes and saw one of the boys come running out. A falling timber seemed to graze him, just barely scraping his head.

But the boy ignored it. He turned and stood as I had, frozen to the spot, staring at the fire with wide-open eyes.

I ran toward him. The heat coming from the house was astonishing. "Evan, are you okay?"

"I'm Max," he said. He was still staring at the fire. He seemed transfixed. Not smiling, exactly—but definitely not afraid.

I grabbed his arm to pull him away and immediately started choking. Black, oily smoke streamed into my eyes, my nose, my lungs. I felt dizzy, sick to my stomach.

"Come on!" I gasped, yanking him away from the house.

I only got a short distance from the house when Max pulled free of my hand. Again he turned to face the house. I turned, too, and got another lungful of smoke. I started to gasp for oxygen. My ears were stinging, tearing. My throat was raw. I couldn't move, couldn't think. Every breath I took made it worse. I fell to my knees and then to the ground.

I glanced up through the billowing clouds of black smoke.

Flames leaped from the upper windows. All except one.

Where's Evan? I thought desperately. I couldn't help fearing the worst.

Then I saw—or thought I saw—the small, sweet face of Evan Willoughby in the upper window. He was crying in terror.

"Hellllp me!" he shouted.

I started to crawl toward the house. I didn't have much hope of making it in time, but I had to try. But just then Laura appeared in the window beside the screaming child. She lifted him up by his armpits, gently.

Good girl, I thought. Lower him out of the window. "I'll catch him, Laura!" I called to her. As if I could.

But instead, she carried him back into the house.

What was she *doing*? "Laura!" I screamed. "No! Wait!"

I forced myself to my feet, stumbled toward the house's door. But an instant later Evan came running out. He ran straight into my arms, crying.

We were both coughing like mad as I hugged him

to me. We made our way away from the house. Evan was running. I was kind of tottering.

It seemed forever before we got far enough to breathe air that wasn't filled with smoke. I sank down against the trunk of a tree. Evan sat beside me, Max a few feet away.

"Are you guys okay?" I croaked. "What happened?"

"I went in the house to play," Evan answered, coughing a little. "And it caught fire. But Laura showed me the way out."

"Laura did?" I looked back at the house. It was completely consumed by flames now.

Evan nodded. "She showed me the steps that weren't on fire."

"But why didn't *she* come out?" I asked quickly. "Where is Laura now?"

Evan's face clouded over, as if he didn't want to think about the answer. In a small, trembling voice he said, "She said she couldn't go with me. She stayed in the fire."

Then he flung himself into my arms and started to cry again. I held him and felt tears running down my own face. Laura had given her life for the boys. I would never see her again. Something inside me felt ripped in two, and I knew it would never completely heal.

I glanced over at Max. He seemed uninterested in

his brother's close call. Instead, he was playing on the ground with some sticks.

Forming them into bundles.

The fire blazed quickly after that. There was a high wind that day, and within minutes, the whole Parr house was gone. As if by magic, it had been reduced to smoke and ashes. Then even the ashes blew away. And I couldn't help wondering what my oxygen-deprived brain had really seen.

By the time Mrs. Willoughby returned, a few moments later, all evidence of the house was gone. There were some scorched branches on the ground as if there had been a small forest fire. Happens all the time.

Mrs. Willoughby ran up the trail, out of breath. There were two police officers with her, and a group of firefighters. I guess they'd seen the smoke from the road.

She grabbed her children in her arms and hugged them so hard I thought she'd break their ribs.

"Evan, Max, my poor babies! Are you okay? What happened?"

Max didn't answer. He just shrugged and pulled away, and went back to his bundles of sticks.

"Max?" his mother called, frowning.

The little boy glanced up. And all at once his mother and I saw it. There was a mark—a deep cut—on his forehead.

It looked just like the one Laura had described to me—one of the symbols that kept appearing in her journal. ᚤ

The Futhark mark for "twin."

"Max!" his mother cried. "What happened to you?"

She ran to look at his wound.

"Nothing," he said, smiling. "A big stick fell and scratched me."

"Does it hurt?" she asked.

"No," he answered. "We had fun."

Mrs. Willoughby looked confused. She turned back to Evan. "Sweetie, what happened? I still don't understand. How did you boys get here?"

My head spun as I waited for the answer. I already knew that Laura had kidnapped them.

And everything else had happened just as Laura had predicted from her vision.

A fire at Rustin Parr's house . . . set by Max . . . with Evan inside.

Except that the ending was different. Evan had survived. Laura had saved him, sacrificing her own life.

She stayed in the fire. That was what Evan had said.

The boys' mother glanced over at Max again. He was still playing with the sticks, forming bundles and strange patterns, with an expression of total concentration.

She repeated her question to Evan. "How did you get here, honey? Tell Mommy."

"We came with the lady," Evan answered.

"With Laura? Did she bring you in the car?"

"No. The old lady," Evan said. "The one with the funny clothes."

Those words shot through me like one of Laura's knives.

It didn't seem possible, but it had to be.

The Blair Witch.

Afterword

I never saw Laura Morely again, not that I really expected to. And to my knowledge, no one else ever did, either.

The next few days were a nightmare. I couldn't sleep. I couldn't eat. And all I kept thinking was, This was my fault. I should have believed her from the start. I should have seen how much danger Laura was in. I should have put her on a plane back to Minnesota as soon as we saw those photographs. Of all people, I should have known just how deadly Black Hills Forest can be.

But I wanted information for my investigation. I wanted Laura to lead me to the truth. And now she was gone.

I had to call Laura's parents and tell them that

she'd been staying with me. I explained that she'd been having strange visions and that she had disappeared in the woods.

I even told them about the fire at the house—a fire at a house that no one believed was there. (All the evidence of a house burning was gone by the time the firefighters got there. I told the chief of the fire department what I had seen, but it was useless. He gave me a song and dance about how smoke inhalation deprives your brain of oxygen. How it can skew your perceptions. How even a small forest fire makes a lot of smoke. I knew all that.)

I also knew what I had seen. And I thought Mr. and Mrs. Morely should know the truth. I don't know for sure whether they believed me, but I had a feeling they did. After all, they knew about the curse.

Evan Willoughby backed me up, but no one paid much attention to him. Was the report of a four-year-old kid suffering from smoke inhalation reliable? Hardly. Children that young often can't tell the difference between fantasy and reality.

But Evan stuck to his story. Whenever someone asked him what had happened, he said the same thing. An old woman had taken them to the woods—not Laura. Then Evan had gone into the house, and it had caught fire. Laura had showed him the way out. Then she'd disappeared.

I tried to get Max to talk. "How did the house catch fire?" I asked him over and over.

He just smiled. Finally he said, "I don't know. It just did."

A full-scale search of the woods ensued, of course, and Sheriff Cravens was just as skeptical this time as he was when Heather disappeared. But he gathered up a search party, and we spent four days looking for Laura, combing the area for any clue.

We never found anything. No sign that Laura had been there—ever.

My car was still parked at the side of the road, but no keys were found inside. I left it sitting there while we searched the woods. I had no choice, since it took a long time to find someone to make a new key. Besides, I had this crazy hope that Laura might be alive somehow—that she had escaped the fire and she'd be back. She might even take the Morris Minor to get away, if that was what she wanted.

She never did.

Finally, the day after the fire, I got an e-mail from Ted the Fed.

```
Cade:
    Sorry it took me so long to get
back to you. I've been out of town
on assignment. Attached are the
files you wanted on Laura Morely. To
```

sum it up, there was only one hospital stay in Minneapolis when she was three years old. Cosmetic surgery to remove a scar. The doc's name was Gregory Appleton, but he seems to have disappeared. I can't locate him. I'll keep trying.

The only other hospital records were the birth certificates for Morely and her twin sister, Stephanie. And then the death certificate for Stephanie. Died two hours after she was born, cause of death: low birth weight and immature lungs. But you probably already knew that.

That's about it. Hope all is well. Keep the Web site burning, kid. And keep in touch.

Later—
Ted

I stared at my computer screen in disbelief. Laura was a twin! She'd never mentioned that fact. Had she even known?

I couldn't quite take all this in. My head throbbed as I read the e-mail over again.

Did that explain Laura's connection to Rustin and Dale Parr . . . her visions about Max and Evan Willoughby . . . ? All of them were twins. And in each set, one of them had died . . . or almost died. And in at least one case, the cause appeared to be murder.

And what about the scars? Laura might have had one, before it was erased by surgery. And now Max had one, too.

What about Rustin Parr? Then I remembered something from Laura's journal. Hadn't one of the voices Laura heard in the woods mentioned some kind of scar?

I mulled all of this over for a while before confronting Laura's parents. I mean, they'd been through a lot already. They'd lost their daughter.

But I had to know: Why didn't they tell Laura that she had a twin?

At first Laura's mother lied, denying that there had ever been a twin.

When I told her I had the medical records, she finally broke down and admitted that, for their own personal family reasons, they'd never wanted Laura to know that her twin had died.

"But what about the scar?" I asked.

"There was no scar," Mrs. Morely insisted. And then she slammed down the phone.

When I tried to reach Laura's parents again a few

months later, they'd moved. Abruptly, according to neighbors, to another state.

So was there some kind of twin curse involved in this case? One evil twin, one good twin?

Was Laura part of that twin curse?

And if so, was she good or evil?

All of that remains unknown.

But here's what I *do* know.

The night of Laura's disappearance I opened her packed bags—the ones she had left sitting in our kitchen. The police would want to look through them—and then mail them back to her parents. I knew they would take her things away. This was my last chance to look through Laura's possessions, to see if they held any answers.

I found the negatives, the ones she had shot in the woods—and I kept them. Weeks later Mr. Mellon helped me print them again, but there was nothing on them now—just rocks and trees and the old house foundation.

I also found Laura's journal.

I read it again, front to back, hoping to find some clues to the mystery of her disappearance.

I found only one.

On a page where she had scrawled a bunch of Futhark symbols and phrases in Transitus Fluvii—something caught my eye.

The words looked different this time. As if they'd changed somehow.

When I translated them again, the message was different. Now it read:

To see too much . . . to save a life.

I stared at the letters. Did I translate them wrong the first time? Copy them wrong? I checked the notes I'd been keeping since Laura had arrived in Burkittsville. No. There was no mistake.

So I've closed the case file on Laura Morely with more questions than answers, as usual.

I still have the hope that she survived. That by saving little Evan from his own twin, she somehow changed the curse of the Blair Witch—and saved not just Evan's life, but her own.

But here's what I've been wondering: Is there something terribly dangerous about being a twin born in Burkittsville? And what if the Willoughby twins' ordeal isn't over yet? Maybe it has just begun. . . .

My greatest concern is the one that I live with day and night: The fear that the evil of the Blair Witch lives on. And that no matter what I do, I may never find a way to understand it—or to defeat it.

WIN A TRiP to the Set of *Blair Witch 3*

OFFICIAL RULES & REGULATIONS

I. HOW TO ENTER

NO PURCHASE NECESSARY. Enter by printing your full name, address, phone number, date of birth, and description of supernatural experience (150 words maximum) on a piece of paper, and mail to BLAIR WITCH 3 CONTEST, Random House Children's Marketing Department, 1540 Broadway—19th floor, New York, NY 10036. Entries must be received by Random House no later than January 16, 2001. LIMIT ONE ENTRY PER PERSON. Partially completed or illegible entries will not be accepted. Sponsors are not responsible for lost, late, mutilated, illegible, stolen, postage-due, incomplete, or misdirected entries. All entries become the property of Random House and will not be returned, so please keep a copy for your records.

II. ELIGIBILITY

Contest is open to all legal residents of the United States, excluding the state of Arizona and Puerto Rico, who are between the ages of 12 and 18 as of January 1, 2001. All federal, state, and local laws and regulations apply. Void wherever prohibited or restricted by law. Employees of Random House, Inc., Artisan Pictures Inc., Parachute Publishing, L.L.C., and their parent companies, assigns, subsidiaries or affiliates, advertising, promotion and fulfillment agencies, and their immediate families, and persons living in their household are not eligible to enter this contest.

III. PRIZE

One Grand Prize Winner will win a trip to the set of *Blair Witch 3*, including airfare, ground transportation to and from set and airport, and a hotel stay for 1 night, for the Winner and one parent or legal guardian. (Approximate retail value $1,000.) Travel and use of accommodation are at risk of Winner and parent/legal guardian, and Random House, Artisan Pictures Inc., and Parachute Publishing, L.L.C. do not assume any liability. If for any reason prize is not available or cannot be fulfilled, Random House, Artisan Pictures Inc., and Parachute Publishing, L.L.C. reserve the right to substitute a prize of equal or greater value, including, but not limited to, cash equivalent. Taxes, if any, are the Winner's sole responsibility. Prizes are not transferable and cannot be assigned. No prize or cash substitutes allowed, except at the discretion of the sponsor due to prize availability.

IV. WINNER

Odds of winning depend on total number of entries received. All prizes will be awarded. One Grand Prize Winner will be chosen on or about February 1, 2001, from all eligible entries received within the entry deadline by the Random House Children's Books Marketing Department. The contest will be judged by staff of the Random House Children's Books Marketing Department, whose decisions are final, and prizes will be awarded on the basis of originality and creativity. The Grand Prize Winner will win a trip to the set of *Blair Witch 3* to see the filming in action. The prize will be awarded in the name of the Winner or the Winner's parent or legal guardian, if a Winner is under age 18. Winner's parent or legal guardian will be notified by mail and Winner's parent/legal guardian will be required to sign and return affidavit(s) of eligibility and release of liability within 14 days of notification. A noncompliance within that time period or the return of any notification as undeliverable will result in disqualification and the selection of an alternate winner. In the event of any other noncompliance with rules and conditions, prize may be awarded to an alternate winner.

V. RESERVATIONS

By participating, Winner (and Winner's parent/legal guardian) agrees that Random House, Artisan Pictures Inc., and Parachute Publishing, L.L.C. and their parent companies, assigns, subsidiaries or affiliates, advertising, promotion and fulfillment agencies will have no liability whatsoever, and will be held harmless by Winner (and Winner's parent/legal guardian) for any liability for any injuries, losses, or damages of any kind to person, including death, and property resulting in whole or in part, directly or indirectly, from the acceptance, possession, misuse, or use of the prize, or participation in this sweepstakes. By entering the contest the Winner consents to the use of the Winner's name, likeness, and biographical data for publicity and promotional purposes on behalf of Random House, Artisan Pictures Inc., and Parachute Publishing, L.L.C., with no additional compensation or further permission (except where prohibited by law). Other entry names will NOT be used for subsequent mail solicitation. For the names of the winners, available after February 15, 2001, please send a stamped, self-addressed envelope to: Random House, *Blair Witch 3* Winners, 1540 Broadway—19th Floor, New York, NY 10036.

WIN

A TRIP to the Set
during the filming of
Blair Witch 3!

✝
™

Experience the horror
of *Blair Witch 3* up close!

Tell us about your brush
with the supernatural in
150 words or less and
enter to win an
all-expense-paid trip to
the set of *Blair Witch 3*.

See official contest rules on opposite page.